# North for Sun

Marie Deaconu-Baylon

© 2017, Marie Deaconu-Baylon. Except as provided by the Copyright Act, no part of this publication may be reproduced, stored in a retrieval system, or transmitted in any form or by any means without the prior written permission of the publisher.

For Cosmin, my favorite book
For Nanay, our story-teller and historian

# Chapter 1

The doctors won't tell me whether anesthesia lets you choose your last thought. The internet won't tell me, either. The video that turns up shows closed eyes and candy-colored buttons. Beeping and more hoses. Her face looks smaller asleep. The scene cuts to an animation of an elegantly spinning brain while the girl's foot shakes. I need to know if consciousness blacks like a curtain or a fading. With my night pill, the unconsciousness came like fast sleep, except for the catches in my breath. I'm used to breathing, so I woke up when I stopped.

When the chair kicks back, the girl closes her eyes and gets a moment of composure. I get very nervous thinking about this moment. I don't trust the way her body lies. It shrinks. My thoughts have ruined a lot of moments for me, and I don't want to start off my new brain on the wrong foot. I don't know if it works that way. No one knows how it works. If I stare at the picture of the lake long enough, it will paint itself on my dark inside eyes. Given a choice, I would like this view for a start, or at least I would choose it over something ugly. Or if they let me have headphones, I'd like that.

After my eyes re-open, I guess I'll be hungry, so I was thinking about packing myself a snack. Something wholesome like an orange. Food hasn't been interesting for a while, but the doctors say I could feel better right away. Anyway, I like knowing what I'll do when I wake up. Nobody knows if I'll be able to write when I wake up, or I don't trust the people who say they know. I know I will be able to read.

My life was hard to weigh until it became easy. I choose a shaking foot over a spinning brain. All my literary machinations aren't worth as much as an orange, enjoyed from the peel to the final segment. If I can have months of eating oranges, I'll give up writing about ugliness. While I can, I squeeze out the words like wringing a rag. Time travel gives me pictures of the past, but I want memories. If I can't remember my voice when I wake up, I'll read it. I'll tell myself how to get better. He'll tell me again and again. Alongside the snack, I fit my small life into the box for after I re-open. I choose something whole for a start.

# Chapter 2

Before I walked, I watched myself in the dressing room mirror, standing with a strange girl I knew for a peripheral castmate for this act: my first return to college. The dining hall was particularly suspicious that day. The strange girl sat at my table, which was feeling too warm in the unnatural lamps. Her expression was sweet as a flower, and I looked forward to the beginnings of things. In the mirror, my reflection retold me this anticipation.

"It's so close, it's almost moving," the girl said about the picture. "I could stare at the lake all day."

The frame swallowed light into its metal. It was striped blue on blue, and the view assured me I was well again. I bought it with a haste that I mixed up with happiness before we left.

The pedestrian street outside the campus bookstore wasn't completely plowed, so we picked our way down the path carved for us. Her flower face couldn't be seen past our heavy coats. She talked about herself urgently. I don't remember her name. I surprise myself with my awful memory. Time travel should give me a special ownership over the past, but it runs away the same.

The picture is on my desk. I can see her face if I try. Her

skin and hair were the same as mine after a summer of fading. Her face was familiar in the way that a friendly face is familiar, or at least it was easier to read the friendliness because I knew her face.

I could hold onto that face. Most faces since the hospital were masks. The plastic bend around the smiles, the angles that changed too fast for real human expression. I became very worried I wouldn't see a person again.

Sometimes I think I would trade everything that followed for this girl. She has become a kind of opening into a more wholesome and linear life, and maybe she was. I can't give some people up. At the end of things, I want to see that our lives ran parallel all along. Whatever afterwards came in the shadow of our meeting, which means we were fixed closer than we thought.

When I finally told Dan about that night, I left her out. It wouldn't be popular to tell my future husband he wasn't the watershed in my life, that he was probably himself a radius from this unnamed girl. I skipped to the walk.

"I walked across Lake Mendota. The entire thing. It was frozen over. I was following the sun."

Dan leaned his elbows across the table. I thought his eyes were bluer, but I couldn't see if they were numb or melting. He is always bending, inspecting things. This dirty bar had grown old with us. I hadn't seen these wrinkles, like fresh slits in ice steadily forking and cross-hatching.

"I know you weren't following the sun," Dan said.

"How did you know?" Sometimes I expected that I hadn't done it at all. If someone proved my life wrong, I'd be relieved for the answer.

"You said it was night when you got to the other side? And you were going north." He scanned the maps behind his eyes. He was leaning too close now, face-first, while he

## Chapter 2

crushed nachos into his mouth. "The sun passed on your left. You couldn't have been walking toward it."

The story had been full of holes. Some I could feel: pits that pulled other memories until the borders fell in. I didn't know the story had a sun-shaped hole. I wouldn't have been surprised if Dan told me I dreamed the whole night and the girl before.

"You must have been confused," Dan said. "It was cold enough to freeze the lake solid, and you never wear a hat. I know you. You were freezing and hungry."

"Of course I was." I didn't explain yet how, on the other side, the confusion was insightful. "It took a long time. I don't know how long. I walked in a straight line the whole way. I thought if I got to the other side, I could do anything."

If he didn't understand that night, he didn't understand me. I had gone back and back to that night until it was a lighthouse on my timeline. I felt my boat shoes, almost slippers, sinking into the snowbank. The land had been brought to me. A lawn ornament, looking like a grounded kite, was spinning madly.

"I finally get to the other side. It's dark by the time I get to land again. And right where I'm standing is a mental hospital. I can't feel my toes, and I'm reading a sign that says, 'Mental Institute.' Can you believe it?"

I waited for the laugh. I had hoped for an island or woods, somewhere I could live in peace, and got an asylum. He couldn't tell me otherwise. On a map, I saw the student union and the hospital connected with a dance pattern of my steps.

"I believe you." He looked past me, as if he was watching the game. He pushed back into the booth cushion that absorbed every old secret, until his shoulders curled. I looked around the bar at people watching. I didn't want to be overheard anymore.

"What happened next? After you got to the hospital?" Dan said.

"I walk up to the front desk and tell the guy I need a ride back to campus," I said. I was already laughing. "Guy sits back, sick of his life. And he gives me a ride back! He asks me in the car what I'm studying." Even the man's beard had been hapless, the few full-grown patches scruffy and silly.

Dan didn't smile. "Nice of him," he said. His eyes left the game or whatever had been past me. They were unsteady. I didn't see any of the meanness I knew how to throw away. "He didn't have to do that."

The story was proof of my cleverness. I had outsmarted a lake and then a professional at his own game of containment. He brought me through the exit, not the door with a buzzer that kept people in. Who made the mistake?

"What are you trying to say?" I said.

Dan's eyes gathered mine. "He probably knew and tried to help you."

"He didn't help me," I said. His help would have inverted the punchline, with me as the ridiculous figure instead of him. "He drove me back to where I started. And what about his job?" I wasn't sure what his job was. I remembered the worker scrutinizing me, behind the desk and later in the rearview mirror.

From my travels, I estimated Dan and I would be married for at least ten years, but I hadn't seen enough to guess what those years were. It really was a good joke. People always laughed. The story represented the attitude toward madness that I deserved. I had earned a break by now.

"Then what happened?" Dan said. "After you got back to school?" He made a fist and knocked on the table.

## Chapter 2

"The police took me to the hospital a couple days later. I guess somebody saw me walking down the freeway."

The story was supposed to close earlier, at the punchline. I knew this ending would wobble Dan's eyes further. He cried. It was like him to miss what I knew, that I had crossed a full earth since that night and kept on. He saw the sickness; he would say in a minute.

But Dan told me the walk had worked, that the sun set north sometimes. He listened to where I went after. I guessed he finally saw all the cracks, how pretty they had been first in sun and then moon, fragmenting the ice a step away from my straight path. I don't know how I didn't fall in.

I decided Dan understood. I don't visit that night anymore, but I still keep the picture over my desk. It's a frozen lake made of flat brushstrokes. It's shabby for a talisman, but it fits my life nowadays, a miniature of that night. The painting looks more like the walk than a photo would. The horizon had been remote as paper when I crossed it. When I got to the other side, I felt like a navigator before maps. At the end, my trip contracted, and I could have walked until morning.

# FALL QUARTER: WRINGING A RAG

# Chapter 3

My second return to college was solid with promises, but they were the kind that tethered and weighed. The palm trees on campus were more beautiful than anything I'd seen in the last year. Their expense reminded me how much I was betting on myself. And I still hadn't figured out how to write. Writing was like trying to summon a ghost. I didn't know where my voice went.

Since my missed connection with the strange girl, I tried very hard to recognize the people who were supposed to be the centers of my life. I knew some faces to watch out for. I saw a girl shadowed at the end of the hall whose movement reminded me of someone. She took up more space than she needed. After my parents left, I found a reason to be around her. With the lights turned up, she did have the same nose but a different atmosphere from my friend. She had less warmth behind the prettiness. I wondered whether twenty years could sharpen her into the woman I had seen in our future. Or if she was someone else completely.

The key lay heavy in my back pocket. I wished for a lanyard to wear around my neck. I'd lost my room key a few weeks into college in Wisconsin. My roommate slept at her boyfriend's, and I didn't have her phone number. Even if I got it somehow, I could barely understand people in person, and the phone's background vibrations made my cousin whisper. Texting required translating my thoughts into shapes, which was another impossibility. Sleeping in strangers' rooms became a way to meet people, but hard floors didn't help my insomnia. Sometimes I asked if I could stay, and other times I pretended to fall asleep until morning.

I was very lucky. Almost all of my roommates had been good in the ways that counted. Nobody stole my stuff or woke me up. My first roommate at Stanford seemed like a happy sort of person, and she didn't bring up the retching noises my throat made in the mornings. My second roommate at Wisconsin didn't eat my food during the odd gap when I was in the hospital. My mother filled out the paperwork for me to drop out, and the box of food I found when I got home was complete. I touched and counted each cardboard box again.

I wish I remembered all my roommates in the hospitals, but some were brief or had fuzzy looks to them. I remember the faces of most of my long-term roommates. They had all kinds of skin and hair. My roommates tended to emerge as the movers and shakers in the unit, and I felt privileged to start and end my days with them. I really think other people got jealous, so I tried to be generous. Thanks to my roommates, I ended up in the cliques with the most laughs and fun. It didn't start out that way, but I got to it after I learned to think and talk. If I could have friends like them, I thought I had something worth knowing in me.

The key wouldn't engage with the lock. It rattled as it turned circles in my hand. It was a bad sign that my new roommate didn't jump to open the door, but maybe she was the kind of person to ignore incompetence as a kindness. I didn't find out because the room was empty. Her things

## Chapter 3

that I could see looked hard and considered, except for a homemade ceramic. It was a brain, the color of soft mud, with a hollow inside for a candle. The handbook said we weren't allowed to have candles, so I guessed she'd put an electric light inside.

I didn't know what to put in my side of the room, other than my lake picture that suddenly looked artsy in the sparseness. My first two college rooms had been jiggered to look like my bedroom at home, but I had seen too much of it in the last year. My roommate had set down a rug whose circumference bumped into our beds, since we were closer than either of us had calculated. Her boxes took on an abandoned look, as if they were empty under the flaps. I heard a knock at the door, and each time I dropped what I was doing to get into position. My roommate's first look would be me in active, vital movement. Sitting cross-legged on the floor showed I was open-minded. I would pick my most interesting box and reach down elbows deep. As she opened the door, I would draw out a homemade ceramic of an eyeball.

I almost closed the door, leaving a crack for only the most motivated to break. The habit started in the hospital, where I learned the exact degree of openness that still demanded a knock. People wandered in like the nurses had, introducing themselves as they started their shifts. I rehearsed the conversation I would have with my roommate. Introductions didn't include diagnosis anymore, and the omission freed and pressured. Hallway sounds of strangers going to dinner carried into my room. The old secret—the comfortable talent for hiding and loneliness—closed around my heart. At the end of the day, I didn't have anything to show for all the people I'd known. They expired in the same way: the friends who crowded my life coming up, and my fellow patients, lovely in our shared transformation. They were all lost with the sickness that had excited my mind, and now the rest felt too close to lifelessness. We thought life kept walking its pattern, that we got to keep and accumulate ourselves. I lay in bed hungry.

She didn't knock. I sat up, and she mistook the rigidity for wakefulness. She said she'd driven to Modesto and back. Her face was blue in the nighttime sky through the blinds. She tried to flip the switch slowly, but it only had two modes. The room brightened without gentleness.

"I'll turn it off in a minute," she said.

Tina leaned against the doorframe as she always would. She frowned as she sometimes would. She wouldn't lose the plant-like slenderness until she got much older. She'd been a cross country champion in high school, so victory burned into her body even when its wiry lines failed. I sweated in a tank top, and her brown skin looked cool to the freckle. The new lights filtered through masses of black hair; her face had a spotty intensity around it. I blinked. It was the youngest I'd ever see, but it was already barely lined. Crinkles jumped out as she smiled, around the eyes whose blackness was the same in all the doors and rooms I knew her.

This was the first room I knew her, so small that I claim every fold in the carpet. If I went back to our room and waited long enough, we'd walk in with the still faces we kept for each other after a long day. I'd listen to our comments and silences, how they relaxed with time until the air itself was companionable. Sometimes we went years without seeing each other. When we did, it was the end of a long day, and our faces stilled again.

"Where have you been?" I asked.

Her parents had been too tired to drive back. Her brother was supposed to help, but he had to take care of things last-minute. She sat on the floor with a box and left things on the

## Chapter 3

floor as she sorted.

"I don't know if you're from California, but it never rains. I can't decide if it's lucky," Tina said. She pulled out an umbrella.

"Did you say you're from Modesto?" I remembered the rehearsals and brought back the script. It was very important to remember people's facts. My memory still slogged, so I drew faces with labeled names in my planner. Strangers liked to talk about places. Our room was either kind of terminus. Now that we were both here, it became an origin for whatever came after. Tina changed from shorts into pants.

"My parents are." She browsed her wallet, counting eight bills and change. "I hope you didn't wait for me to eat. It's a mistake if you did." She looked at my transparent stomach. I wanted to puff it out until it became round with fullness and initiative.

"I really am sorry I woke you up." She threw a purse on her shoulder and remembered her keys on the desk. Her hand waited on the light switch. "You'll see, I'm a good roommate."

"I know." I had lost enough friends to know the feel of danger, and Tina felt flat. She'd be predictable, whether or not she wanted me. I needed boundaries I could count on, so I'd know to stay away.

"Do you want to come? I was thinking of finding food." Her shadow was elegant in the door.

After a year of being led from place to place, walking alongside somebody took force and thrust. I watched my feet. The rain was too light to make puddles. Tina kept closing her umbrella to test the drops. She didn't check a map as we crossed from garden to the next garden. The accumulation of near-motionless months creaked my legs.

Even though they scared me at first, the trees made me better. And the colors. It was true that I had to clench my teeth to hold in vomit the first time around. But something about this night, breathing the same thin air as my new roommate, gave me a snug feeling. Maybe it was because I avoided leaving my room after nightfall during my first freshman year, so the view as we ran was a new perspective. Most things are better blurred with rain. I still remember wiping drops from my eyes over and over, until the library's horrible awning looked like warm invitation. The next day, when the sky cleared and the sun came out, I found I recognized it all. With time, I learned to enjoy the inside places, too, the stones baked to sand and smudged windowsills. I think if I tried, I could say every tree in the place, or at least know them if I met them again.

"My brother went here, so I know campus pretty well," Tina said. "It's big, but it makes sense."

The cashier jumped when we interrupted his peace. A girl walked in and out for a bag of potato chips in one stride. We'd lament this store every time, for its empty smell and shelves of soup and old apples, without anything a person could live on after graduation. Tina wouldn't pay cents for a plastic bag. I locked my fingers around all ends of the egg carton, pinching it safely until my knuckles whitened. The shadows of palm trees clawed into the air like bats, but we sailed against them until home.

"Don't you know how to crack an egg?" Tina asked. She swished banana slices into a frying pan. The kitchen smelled like sugar and butter, the beginnings of holidays. She cored apples; they crunched.

The shell shattered, and the snot was cold in my hands. I stared at it too long. The cold was invigorating. "I haven't cooked in a while."

Tina took the eggs I'd cracked and squished them into

yolk and white. She chunked doughnuts. The caramel bubbled, filling the room with toffee.

"What's your major?" I said.

Tina's arm flexed as she stirred whites into foam. The microwave beeped, and she whipped eggs and sugar into melted ice cream. The doughnuts drowned in the custard.

"I'm going to be a brain surgeon." She would be a chemist and finally a chef. I tried to think of another question.

"I guess your hobby is pottery," I said. "I saw the brain sculpture candle. It's really nice."

"My mom made it." She stuffed doughnut pudding where the apple cores had been, laying caramelized bananas on top. I opened the oven door for her to slide the apples inside.

"I'm really tired tonight. I wish we met on a different day. I do want to get to know you tomorrow," Tina said.

I had asked about her parents for the first time. I spooned foam unevenly over the stuffed apples.

"You don't know me yet, but I don't get disappointed," Tina said. The lighter faltered before it caught, and she torched until the meringue went gold. "It's not like you get another first day of college, and I missed it."

She made a face and cursed the lack of cinnamon. My teeth could have broken from the deliciousness. I couldn't remember a better meal. Tina insists she made a savory course. She doesn't believe me how good it was, especially since I forgot the main dish.

"People don't think about other people," I said. I ate fast. "Nobody cares if you missed it. Nobody can tell."

We woke up and went to our second breakfast. The forty freshmen in my dorm would get into a habit of eating at three round tables. Depending on the side, we had views of the garden or the soft-serve machines. When we started, the cast rotated as if on a turntable. People who would later seem incongruent standing near each other ate together, and everyone wanted variety. It was all exciting. I wasn't good at this arrangement. One girl occasionally wore glasses, which made me reintroduce myself each time as if she was new. I wanted us to settle into our relationships. But I would miss the equality of the turntable. At graduation, I said good-bye to my dorm-mates as if we had never been separated at all, and those weeks had been years.

After a few weeks, I remembered how to write, but I didn't have anything to say. I worked very hard on a short story about a woman falling asleep on a plane. In Philosophy classes, I learned I could take other people's voices. Time travel was unhelpful because, being a brown woman, I wouldn't have been allowed to talk in the past. I didn't talk much in the present, either. I liked knowing my classmates were almost as confused as me.

Since I was scared of missing people, I agreed to almost every social invitation. I ended up watching movies I had already seen, eating hot dogs at games, and, once, staying in the shallow end of the pool since I can't swim. I floated on my back. I drank and danced. In this spirit of sociality, I went with Tina to choir auditions.

"Watching is boring," she said as we biked over. We merged into a roundabout. Upperclassmen called it the Intersection of Death, so we did, too. It wasn't an intersection anymore. I never forgot how to ride a bike.

"I don't think I'll get bored," I said. I'd learned to turn off my brain when I met new people.

"It's too long to wait. Most people aren't good singers," Tina said. "It'll be fun. You might meet someone."

She knew how to convince me to go out. The audition hall was our dorm stage amplified: four times as many steps

# Chapter 3

and a bigger piano. I wasn't sure if there was a size after grand. I couldn't count how high the ceiling was, but it was all much too circular. I watched the noise, tangling into deadly knots, rise higher and higher until it bumped into the dome forever. The only person I knew was Tina, and she looked like she knew a lot of people. I searched the room for my people as I always did.

Time travel left me with an exhausting mental calculus. I had shuttled back and forth so many times that I had an almost psychic grip on cause and effect. I had seen a lot of history, so I knew what was coming next in most situations. I could read signals and follow them.

That day, I saw all the cues. The crowd was too still for its number, and everyone stuck to their marks. I knew the stillness was making room for something awful. The room sang with people warming up. The sound thinned until no one wanted to be the only voice. Judges filed in. Tina went quiet and damned us with silence.

"Good luck, babe," Tina said. She squeezed my hand. Her sentimentality had to be another sign.

The groups would sing together and then individually. The judges represented different choirs and would fight over us after the audition. I tracked Tina's ponytail until the mob closed over.

Once I saw all the signs, I couldn't be sure what to do. With time traveling, I don't get past the picture I'm given. It's not an exact picture, more an awareness with extra-sharp sides. Too constrained to be useful. At the auditions, I didn't see what end I was trying to avoid or fulfill. I knew I needed to get out of whatever awful was on its way, so I decided to act unpredictably. I'd dodge for as long as I could. I braced myself.

"I'm Martha Marcelo," I said. Nobody had asked. I

introduced myself too many times for the size of the group. People looked surprised, which was a good sign. I must have been on the right track.

"I'm singing 'Feeling Good.' I really relate with it, so I'm choosing it. I'm feeling good right now, here."

Was it unpredictable enough? I couldn't figure out how to sing unpredictably. Was I supposed to sing the wrong tune, too? I lobbed my voice a little more than usual. The trumpets or whatever didn't come in on time, which threw me. I didn't need to find the notes that a heart breaks to because they were already there.

I didn't need to hear Tina to know she would make it. I couldn't tell which voice she was, but I imagined her face. Some people think Tina's efficiency is not far from joylessness, but they've never seen her sing. She sang sometimes to whatever kid appointed himself dorm pianist for the day. When she sings, her face drops whatever hardness lives inside. She looks a lot like her brother when she sings.

Tina yelped to open our door in the morning. We heard them for days before they came, pounding doors down our hall for all the clubs. Signs, with membership written in squishy paint, sprouted on people's doors. Tina wore her coolest pajamas every night to impress her choir when they came for her. Screaming, Voices of Reason fell into our room in similar pajamas. The blues and soul choir. Tina cried when she got her envelope. I guess everybody was overcome. Assuming I wasn't needed, I had stayed in bed. A girl with another envelope walked around our laundry to my bedside. Tina hugged me with real tenderness, and I was touched that she wasn't surprised at my admittance.

Acting unpredictably was hard to replicate. My admittance had been unpredictable, so it must have been the less awful end. The others found out I only knew one blues or

## CHAPTER 3

soul song, which I already sang at auditions.

Voices of Reason met twice a week in the basement of a dorm on the other side of campus. I got used to the hike. I had lived at this dorm my first freshman year, and the building was older than where I lived with Tina. The ivy walls that used to choke me now climbed. The staircase wasn't a condemned spiral at all. When I walked through the glass doors, I thought my life was opening up again.

"The freshmen are so quiet. Haven't you been to West Campus before?" Marsha, our president, said. My awe showed. The group respected Marsha for her powers of silence. Her singing voice was plastic in its rising and falling, but she saved her talking voice for the hardest words. Her face, pink and blond, was exactly symmetrical, which added to her unsettling effect. She had a reflected mole at either ear lobe.

"I've been here before," I said.

Tina nodded. Her singing was as lovely as her talking: energetic in places I didn't notice in the written score. "This isn't day one," she said.

Marsha moved on, her footfalls equally pressured from her same-length legs.

Singing felt like reading, like we were emptying and filling at the same time. I used to dance. Dancing meant I couldn't watch the dance, which is what I loved more. Singing was different, and, hearing some songs, my eyes emptied and filled. I learned how to sway like the others did, joined the clapping that felt at first forbidden. I thought I sounded good, a little growly from a year of disuse.

Even with the music, my friendship with Tina progressed more slowly than friendships in the hospital. After two months, I knew her as well as I had known my roommates of two weeks. The hospital suspended our lives in the same place. As patients, we had to wear our breakdown, and the breakdown meant that we belonged to each other. In college, people wore their public selves. We didn't need to protect each other, so we didn't need to care as much. I didn't lie. I was free in telling everyone the outline, but I liked to think I shared it with polish. With the time travel, I was more guarded because I hated the favors people asked when they found out. I learned to make it clear that I didn't have time for favors. My closest friends were exceptions. Tina in particular was always losing her phone. It was easy enough to go back and retrace her steps.

# Chapter 4

The long walk across Lake Mendota left my legs unusable for weeks. I couldn't get out of bed. The nurses tried. They got mad. They said I shouldn't have walked down the freeway without my legs. The man in my head or ears agreed. I heard intent garbling in my ears when I was awake. It was the voice of the grizzle-bearded man who had driven me back to campus. For now, the sounds were incomprehensible, but I dreaded waking up sometime to ordered words. The doctors mistook sleeping for compliance. They discharged me on the condition that I attend daily therapy group.

"I need you to promise me that you'll go to group every day," the doctor said.

My mother promised. I had met the doctor the day before. Something about his cheekbones alerted my mother that he was half-Filipino, and her belief in mental illness had surged in the last hour.

"It's important to exercise your brain while it's healing," the therapy group leader said. Her face bones angled, cruelly. "Boost your cognitive function. Keep your memory healthy, and your mood will be healthy, too. Group therapy is for your body and mind. Work your muscles, learn a new language. Math is the universal language."

## North for Sun

She pointed at squares of construction paper laid out on the basketball court. The sidelines stretched. Each of us crouched to choose a black marker before they rolled away.

A shadow person, either an intern or an interloper, nodded. She was around my age and had her hair in heavy white braids. She was a heap of rags, all nubby fabrics and knit cape. Her identification badge, worn around her neck on a lanyard braid, was cardboard. She would try to change my life.

I took a break, leaning on the bruises on my knees and elbows. I wasn't sure where they came from. I counted. The papers formed a square of nine by nine squares. A boy's sweatpants rode up as he bent, exposing a black stain on his ankle: a tattoo of an oil spill. The ink shined as if it was new. I would have liked to be comfortable in sweatpants. Nobody told me we could wear pajamas.

"Remember, no talking," the group leader said. She and the shadow person sat on the bleachers, knees spread as coaches in strategy.

My lips tasted of oil. The grid made a half-blank calendar. The six of us broke out to study the scattered numbers. I felt distant judgment, and I looked at the intern staring. I didn't know whose eyes had caught the others. She licked her lips.

A woman, identical to my professor, held up a fist and then fingers. The boy stooped and wrote a number. I nodded. Nodding was a good feeling. The boy and my professor waited to write until I nodded. We weren't allowed to talk, so I couldn't explain. I was their shadow person.

When the time ran out, we stepped back and looked at the whole grid. It didn't add up. On one square, someone had drawn my face. I had curves from the sides of my nose to the ends of my mouth. A face in a face, like a monkey. I smiled at it.

The intern collected the sheets of wrong numbers, including my face. She waited for me. I walked faster until I closed in on the eyes.

"I think I tried to hurt myself," I said.

Other group members pushed past us for the double doors.

"I'm glad you're okay," the shadow person said. Her eyes weren't empty.

After I realized what I had done, I remembered Sudoku was popular at my high school last spring. The group leader was right. Remembering was good exercise. Our calculus teacher allowed us to complete the games during class. I won again and again. I think we got interested before the puzzles started appearing in newspapers because Heidi hadn't heard of them yet. I was the older cousin, but she beat me to most things: friends, beauty, calculus. And sanity.

Heidi introduced Sudoku to her differential equations class, but they were too old for games. She got disappointed because it was too easy to beat people her age, so she emailed me puzzles she made herself. When I tried her homemade puzzles, I had to trust that she constructed the squares correctly. Her numbers anchored mine. If my numbers didn't add up, I kept erasing. She never made an error, but her puzzles were very difficult. Sometimes she left too many squares blank.

"Hi, girl," the inked boy said. "You can take that off now." He waved his wrist.

"I couldn't figure it out," I said. The tag from the hospital wouldn't come off. I had tried to soften the yellow band in the shower first, but it wouldn't rip. I lost interest and was afraid to use scissors anyway.

When it was my turn for introductions, I tried to summarize my present state.

"I want to be alone," I said. I thought about what Heidi

would say. "I would say I'm feeling about a 7 out of 10."

The boy nodded. "Welcome to group," he said. "It's hard at first. Keep coming, and you'll see. It gets easier. We've all been in your shoes."

At our kitchen table, I tried to recreate the puzzle on a single square of paper. I drew my face in the right box and smiled at it.

"I'm not going back," I told Heidi on the phone. "I'm younger than everyone else." I didn't mention the boy.

"It's up to you. Honestly, Martha, it sounds ridiculous," Heidi said. "Why did they make you do Sudoku anyway? What's the point?"

I imagined her doing math with her other hand. Heidi would wear her beanie that she wore indoors during winters. San Jose was too warm to justify the heater. Their house wasn't made for damp days. It was a house for sun. As long as I didn't go outside, I was warmer in Wisconsin.

"It's important to remember," I said. I read each square to Heidi. She hummed.

She should have finished the puzzle by now. I won at my school, but she won everywhere. Heidi is so sweet-faced that my family still opens gatherings with memories of her baby roundness. I started out thinking we were the same, but I saw in time that her intelligence was more affectionate than mine. She didn't have my secretiveness. She could talk to anyone about anything, say the most frightening things with that tranquil voice. Nobody was scared of her. She inherited her voice from her father, my *tito*.

"And you're not sure which boxes were filled out at the beginning?" Heidi said. The numbers flipped in her mind, an unwinding calendar.

I examined the squares. "I'm not sure."

## Chapter 4

"I don't know if you can finish it then," Heidi said sadly. "You can't rule out possibilities."

She didn't trust my puzzle. I always loved Heidi more than she loved me. I dragged the stolen black marker. An oil spill ate the calendar.

"What are you going to do if you don't go back?" Heidi said. "Are they going to make you go?"

"I'll work at the Blue Beluga Inn. It's on the ocean." I had researched their website. The bunk beds would be good practice for when I returned to college. It was a train ride away from Stanford, so I could acclimate to the culture of the region.

"If you're coming to the Bay Area, you're staying with us," Heidi said. "I can drive now, so we'll go out. Ma will cook." I heard her work on the half-spilled calendar. She had lied that it was hopeless.

"I need to work at the Blue Beluga," I said. "The pay's not great, but you get free room and board."

"You can stay with us for free," Heidi said. "What do you need to work for?"

"I have to be more independent," I said.

"Come live with me and Mom for a couple months. We have the extra room since Dad's gone. I'd be happy to see you."

I considered my mother's promise to the doctor. "We can try it." I filled in the box for each day I could remember. The numbers shrunk around the spills.

My mother hesitated to break her word to a countryman, but she'd been encouraging me to cheer myself up and felt I was now taking her advice. Scott would glom onto one of us as usual. As long as I can remember, he always winked when he did something nice, as if kindness was sneaky. I thought, after years of cohabitation with us, he'd lose the winking and be fatherly with a straight face. But he couldn't ever be nice to me plainly. My mother thrilled at any show of his pretend parenting, so he made a show every time. She liked his special favors, called them loyalty. She doesn't see that adoration is too desperate.

"The weather could be good for you," my mother said. "If you took better care of yourself, you'd feel much better. You have to have a purpose."

I rubbed my feet. They tingled from the Sudoku memory restoration exercise. I didn't know I had neurons all the way to my toes.

"Working could be the best thing for her right now," Scott said. "Every kid should have a job. Haven't I been saying that for a while? School isn't everything."

He winked at me. I waited.

"Don't forget you are a guest in their house. They will be unhappy if you sleep all the time," my mother said. "You have to wake up, know what you're going to do. Set your mind to it. Write it down. You know how."

"I know how."

"You can help Heidi with her homework while you're with them," my mother said. "You can help her with college applications for next year. It will be a big help to your Tita May." She nodded at my step-father and me. I couldn't tell who the shadow person was.

The bracelet from the hospital had stretched enough that I eased it off. It left a tender band of paler skin underneath. I jabbed at its softness with a fingernail and watched the indentations bounce back.

# Chapter 5

If you get to keep your memories, days in the locked unit feel unrepeatable, at least the first time. Being mutually trapped bonded us, and each patient's exit felt like the end of a special life. As we earned discharge, we watched each other gain and lose parts. In the hospital, we knew that all of us would remember this time if we could.

On this count, my friendship with Tina was uncertain. Some people remembered their freshman roommate, and some hardly did. Singing changed things between Tina and me. We approached the constant shared activity that I'm sure attached patients in the hospital: therapy groups, meals, social events, and the craft room. Tina and I now had sleeping, studying, eating, and singing.

The closest Tina and I came to leaving our public selves that first year was when her brother visited.

One thing I don't like about Tina is that, because she skips decisions, she assumes other people can. I was trying to get together the conviction to go to class; there were simply too many of them. For me, the consequences were too great to make any decision lightly. I used to put sticky notes around the house with reminders. Things like, "You want to be outside," "You like food," et cetera. Tina wouldn't understand these notes because, even compared to everyone else, smoothness moved along with her. If she felt any pain, it wasn't a kind that the rest of us could see.

Since Tina doesn't need opportunities to express herself, she didn't give me a chance to struggle with her brother visiting. Once the decision was done, I really wanted to feel like I would have chosen it, too. Selfless is something I would like to be, if I could let go of myself enough to get energy for it. I guess I thought I'd have longer to let go.

"Everyone loves Victor," Tina said. "This is going to sound corny, but he's got a light around him or something. I feel dumb for saying it. When we were growing up, he was my best friend."

Superlatives make me suspicious, especially from Tina. "I can't wait to meet him," I said. I was in bed, which is where I lived when Tina came and went. Being in bed made me feel vulnerable, like I was exposed or compromised or something, so I often felt vulnerable our freshman year.

"Thank you so much for letting him visit," Tina said. "It'll only be a few days. He's got a couple auditions in the city. Then he'll go to our parents' place until he hears back."

I held onto this feeling that Tina and I were conspirators sharing a trust. And maybe their closeness could enfold me, too.

I returned from class expecting the routine hours of loneliness until Tina came back. The key slipped. The door was already unlocked. Tina wouldn't have to explain her visitor because the two looked alike as blood does. They could have been the same person except his skin was deeper brown, and his eyes shined like fresh-flowed ink. The brain candle glowed. He'd brought a duffel bag, which he tucked under the windowsill as if the spot had been reserved for it. Victor himself filled the room and threatened to burst it.

## Chapter 5

"How was your trip?" I said. "Did you drive here okay?" I hoped it had been long and interesting. Tina, silent for once, stood next to him with a happiness I hadn't seen. I wondered what it meant if her private self was the happy one.

"Too long. But it was fine, quiet. I've made the drive a lot, so it's always fine," Victor said. "I really appreciate that you're letting me stay here, Martha. I'm sure Tina didn't give you a choice." His smile, even when he's not smiling, grips people.

"Of course. I'm happy you're here," I said.

He opened the window, which faced the wall on the opposite side of the courtyard. The wall was pocked with holes the size of needle heads.

"It's weird to be back, but Tina didn't give me much of a choice, either," Victor said. "I forgot how beautiful it is. You guys should know it's special here." He talked like someone who had been places. I hadn't been anywhere in a long time, and he talked like it was mine.

"I really like it here," I said. It was the first time I believed it. "You can move my things around if you need to make room." I didn't feel very generous offering our rug, but Victor's thanks made me generous.

I had prepared myself to cameo in Tina's picture of college life. I practiced comfort that I didn't have, pointing out the showers like I had always regularly showered. He turned out to be unimpressed, except for a nostalgia that made us feel young. "I used to buy ramen by the crate," he said. He was unimpressed but not disinterested. Mostly, he sounded affectionate for his forgotten, laid-aside leavings. Sometimes he was grossed out, but our room was cleaner than most. His kindness disarmed us, when I had expected to be judged. His reminiscences made us feel silly and beloved. We were living a time that would become silly and beloved. It felt serious to us now.

In Victor's character, I saw he had hammered the poles of Tina's personality, the thoughtfulness and mettle, into an alloy like steel. He was five years older than us, and I wondered if Tina would find the same peace.

Victor needed little maintenance. In fact, we wanted him around more than he was. He hadn't spent a whole day with us since the first day when Tina and I skipped class.

"I wish it was a nicer day out, but you've seen it all anyway," Tina said.

I thought a misty day was the best weather to see campus. Its extravagance was as lush but more familiar than the postcard it became in the sun. Gardens jumped out of the gray. The pillars and paving stones shone with rain. We didn't have much interesting to say that needed to be said, especially since Victor knew campus as well as we someday would. "This is the Quad." "The sandwiches here are good." We saw everything interesting.

"Tina, you did okay. Covered a lot of ground, didn't miss out on major stops," Victor said at lunch. He ate a waffle with a tree stamped on it. "I'm going to show you guys the real tour."

"I showed you everything," Tina said. "I guess there's the hospital, but the building's not the good part."

She could have given us a tour of the building. She studied in the medical school library and in the lobby next to families waiting for news. When I would go to the emergency room, she passed me through the automatic doors to tell the other doctors her evaluation.

"I thought we were pretty thorough," I said.

Victor told us about underground tunnels, secret eating spots, sunrise balconies, libraries sparkling with gems, hidden mansions, jungles. Mostly about how to break into places, the times and doors and tools. He started out with journalistic descriptions but, by the end, he had worked up real animation. He laughed at his memories.

"We've been here for months. We don't need you to tell us all the secrets," Tina said. "Save some for us. Show us your favorite place."

We curved down inefficient paths, lined with buzzed grass. Victor tried to point out secrets along the way, but Tina cut him off.

"Over there is the best—"

"Victor!"

"That's the forbidden—"

"Seriously, stop talking."

The circular bench looked more solid than the columns in the Quad, which were embossed with intricacies that would eventually wear down into scratches. The bench stood low to the ground and brought our knees too high when we sat on opposite ends. All shapes of green, carved hedges and cultivated wildness, crept out of corner gardens.

"I don't know what to call this place. I don't know how it works, but I have an idea," Victor said.

"Don't tell us," Tina said.

He lowered his voice. His mouth moved, and his voice conducted in whispers, straight to my ear. The garbling was as close as when it had been in my head. When I covered my ears, it stopped. I understood what the voices were telling me.

"I figured it out. It's in the walls, not the bench. It's the big wall behind us. It's in the acoustics. Like in a museum." The wall jumped into suspicion at her voice. It was a circle's face.

"But there isn't any ceiling here," I whispered. The ceiling in my hospital rooms had been pitted Styrofoam. When I stared up from bed, the voices sank into the mouse holes.

"The walls are high enough. It doesn't matter." He pointed at the side of the building. Overhang from one tree covered the gap to the church's roof.

"It's echoes," I said.

The voices outside my head dragged the voices inside. I couldn't understand them. If I shut my ears and eyes, I thought they stopped, but they were only collecting breath. Victor and Tina whispered. I locked my neck and stared at the sky, tried to make a healthy face. The tree branches fanned as an electric one, like plastic blades. The church had no texture. The walls lost their stones. A lamp lit the plants, made unfitting shadows. I wouldn't look at their faces, couldn't live if I saw dough where I knew was skin. I sat on my hands, pressing the skin into cracks, wishing for more to wake me up.

"Martha, are you okay?" Victor's voice had no urgency, so I heard him past the insistent tones, or memories of tones. He set a hand on my shoulder and smiled. I could feel his hand.

"Let's go back," Tina said. "I can barely hear you." She got up and led us the ways that she knew.

Victor had brought even less than we thought because his duffel bag held instruments. Bronze gleamed, and silver winked. "I'm not staying long," he said. The remaining space fit a couple changes of clothes.

"I brought your flute, Tina," Victor said. Tina played something evasive. The low and high notes unspooled, like they were inventing themselves. She looked surprised at the escaping sound. "You're still good!" Victor said over the music.

When my depression hit the year before, I bought four hundred songs as my last act of rebellion. I burned through

## Chapter 5

each track to find a moment of pleasure. When I reached the last track and felt nothing, I knew that the walls were falling. At these evenings with Victor and Tina, I realized I should have tried jazz. The metals fell on my ear like balm. Our room was too small for the music, and I sat in the sound.

Around this time, Tina and I felt an abundance when we were alone together. Victor could come into the room at any minute, which made us feel that our conversations were rare as a secret. We said more in less time than we ever had. Sentences were suddenly fascinating. I thought that real confidence could come along with this atmosphere of confidence, and I watched for it.

"Victor's a really good musician," I said.

"Victor doesn't know what he's doing, but he'll figure it out," Tina said.

I perked up. Talking about Victor behind his back was maybe an actual secret.

"He's the smartest person I know," Tina said. "If he'd go to more auditions, I know he'll make it. Until then, he can't get lazy."

I sat up in bed with intention and drive. I agreed.

"He doesn't understand our parents like I do. Whatever you give them, it's never enough. They see how nice he is, and they take advantage. I'm not nice like him."

"I think you're nice."

"Thanks, Martha. You don't know me, though."

I'd gotten mixed results, which was my usual harvest with Tina.

Victor's visit showed me that I cared about Tina more than I thought. Before Tina, I never had a friend who didn't need me. She emphatically didn't need me. Didn't she tick off classes like she was punching into a typewriter? She moved people around like they were nothing. And I saw her enough to know that her endurance was no show. She slept soundly at night. She rose each morning imprinting her schedule and everyone else's. When I was depressed, she brought food to our room. She carried our two meal trays and turned the key on her own, too. I slept away the jammed loop in my brain and woke up to salad, soup, and pizza.

Victor had stayed four days when Tina started needing me.

"Martha, I know this is too much to ask," she said as soon as she returned from class. Her question entered the room before she did, through the opening door. It was hard to predict what Tina would consider too much to ask. She could be talking about borrowing a textbook. I remembered the salads, soups, and pizzas, and I thought she could borrow anything.

"Victor needs a place to stay," Tina said. "My parents aren't good people." I was too thrilled by her confidential tone to reflect on what a not good person did.

"What do you mean?"

"They're sucking him in. And he's too nice, so he lets them slide. It's not good for anybody."

"I could ask my aunt," I said. "She's right in San Jose." It made more sense. He could have a room in a house, instead of the leftovers of one-third of a room. I hoped Tina would read the unwillingness in my offer.

"I meant here," Tina said. She wasn't annoyed. She held other people too lightly to get annoyed. Usually, she overwrote the iron in her eyes with kindness, but she looked at me now with unhidden nerve.

"You could talk to Kara. Did you try that?" Kara was a very nice choir member who lived nearby. Sudden affection for Kara shot out of my eyeballs. She was very nice, nicer than I was.

## Chapter 5

"I already asked her. She can't. She has four roommates," Tina said. I hated Kara.

I didn't have enough credit to decline Tina outright. I could carry on about the space and time, but I fast-forwarded to her responses. "He doesn't need much space. You've seen how he is." "It would be a week or so. He's going on so many auditions. You've seen him going, Martha."

Tina didn't keep track of the credits and debits like I did. She probably didn't remember the number of trays. I liked to think I kept track in order to do right by other people. I had too many debts. Sometimes I avoided people to avoid repayments I couldn't afford. It was a small and spiteful self-reliance. Tina didn't care about the ledger. She would have done right by me no matter what I did.

I had carried on enough. I could be generous. "We can try it."

"Thanks, Martha. Now we just have to convince Victor."

She was asking too much.

Tina planned to intervene at Victor's best mood, which I thought made sense. Then, we would whip up his nostalgia, which also seemed doable. Tina would strategize from there whether Victor was ready for the real reasons why he should stay or the fake reasons.

"Okay, so we're going to make music, agree to play all his favorite songs," Tina said. Our time alone had become a true secret. "Then you're going to sing a little. He has a terrible voice, so he loves hearing people sing. Be humble about it, don't show off. Be cool. We'll take a break and give him these nachos. Then, I'll need to make an executive decision. Don't forget the plan. Feel free to improvise."

I really hoped it wouldn't be a night when other dormmates knocked on the door. It made me shudder on a good day, and I needed to be on my game. Victor came back from an audition with a glum face. He said his hands had been too cold from the fog. I wondered whether we were supposed to abort the operation, but Tina signaled to press forward. She was right. Swinging from sorrow to fun seemed to elevate Victor. The relief put him in a humanist mood, like he was nostalgic for his previous sadness. I sang a little. Even with the pressure, the music made it hard to feel burdened.

"I really love it here, with you guys," Victor said. He crunched on the nachos. "The time went so fast. I can't believe I'm going back tomorrow already."

"I love it when you're here, too," I said. "It really did fly by." Tina smiled at me with furtive approval.

"I found a lot of auditions happening next week," Tina said. It was a neutral beginning. I couldn't tell her script yet.

"Oh, yeah? What for?"

"Mostly jazz groups, a kind of chamber ensemble, some stuff teaching kids," Tina said.

"I don't think I'd be a good teacher at all." Victor frowned.

"Like I said, mostly jazz stuff," Tina said.

"Okay. Well, maybe I should go for it. I don't know, though. I told Mom and Dad I was coming back tomorrow. They're probably expecting me."

Tina's hands tightened around her flute, tensed like it was a baseball bat.

"You sound ridiculous. They don't care about you. Why don't you stay with your friends? Mom and Dad are so excited one of us can stand them. They're never going to let you go. It's not good for them, either."

Victor's eyes lazed. His face slackened, unhooking from her crisis. "I don't know. It's not like that, Tina. They're trying."

## Chapter 5

"A lot of people go back and forth between Palo Alto and San Francisco," I said. "If you buy a train pass, it'd be really easy to get around. You're already here." Victor nodded, too promptly. He already knew it all.

"Tina said there's an audition for a jazz bar by the Presidio. It has a balcony. They perform outside sometimes."

Victor and Tina's eyes widened to identical roundness. Tina bobbed her head at me.

"By the ocean?" Victor said. "Damn, that is a good spot."

"It's supposed to be a speak-easy," Tina said. "They do a lot of improvisation. It's their specialty."

Victor started practicing. He wondered whether he should borrow Tina's flute. He preferred saxophone, but it sounded like the kind of crowd that wanted a more off-beat sound. If the place had a drum set or piano ready, he could play them, too. He wished he'd brought his bass, but he was sure they already had a bass. When Victor thanked Tina, I saw that he was the same as me. We were both beneficiaries of Tina's forgiveness program. The music was almost enough.

The first clue came in my German Idealism lecture. I turned over the prepositions between propositions and came up with shiny. Someone in my class talked, and I couldn't see her hands. I pressed my own hands together. They looked like hands and felt like bug belly. I did like I learned in the hospital and sensed my ass on the chair. All that shit from therapy group really works! I imagined the glassy faces of interns reading scripts at us, who sensed our asses in chairs. Why aren't the roads straighter around here? Why don't I have a bike?

"Thesis, antithesis, synthesis. Being, nothing, becoming," the professor said. "Opposing ideas unite without losing themselves. Can anyone think of an example?"

"Maybe like two people who are related to each other

but unique? If those people had offspring who were genetically viable?" I said. "I guess the recessive genes would lose themselves, though. Darn. Maybe like when you cut jelly beans in half to make a new flavor?" Nobody laughed. They all thought I was being serious.

# Chapter 6

I told Heidi to drop me off at the Blue Beluga Inn in San Francisco. I reminded her I must return to Stanford in six months, which meant I needed every penny from my earnings at the Blue Beluga. I wanted to pay my own way through college this time, so I wouldn't need to see Scott again. He made me throw up too frequently. I couldn't miss my first day on the job, or I'd drop out of the Blue Beluga, too.

Since I didn't know my way around, Heidi drove me to her house in San Jose before I noticed. I was too used to mislaid plans to be upset. A private shower would be nicer than the communal bathrooms at the Blue Beluga anyway. My hair had started attracting dust. When it got to this sticky point, I liked to rinse it in very cold water for several seconds. Heidi apologized for the reroute. She warned me that Tita May was extra excited about my visit this time. She wanted to feed me, and she'd cooked for weeks. I wondered what my mother had told Tita May, but then I remembered nothing mattered. I practiced chewing, phantom food slopping around in my mouth like old times.

"Welcome back, my dear!" Tita May said. Her slippers flopped down the entry hall. She sniffed my ears and hair as she hugged me. "Look at you! You lost weight. You look really great. Come, come." She took my bag from Heidi and set it down.

Tita May's black dress hit the floor in a skinny line. Physically, she was a pinched version of my mother. When they stood next to each other, she and my mother were an accelerated timeline of feminine beauty standards. My mother's body was the Jazz Age, fleshy and warm. Tita May stood as chic as a teenage triathloner. She didn't exercise. Neither did my mother. Tita May's hugs were slippery.

"Go rest now before dinner," Tita May said. "I'm still cooking. You eat late at your house anyway. I know. Are you hungry already?" She smacked her lips close to my cheek.

"I'm not hungry," I said. I practiced chewing again. Tita May took my hands.

"My god, Martha, we really needed you," she said. "We are only two in this house now." She waved Heidi at my bag before padding away toward the smell of garlic.

The darkened entry became stairs and a second dim hall. Everything was steep, even floor I knew to be level. I didn't know where all the lights went. I asked for them.

"You'll have to sleep in Dad's old office," Heidi said. "I hope it's not weird for you." The carpet squeaked when she set down my bag.

The room looked like it was made from dusty floorboards. We stepped into the smell of perfumed wood. Two bookshelves held encyclopedia sets in many editions. With each edition, the spines changed colors and emblems from pineapples to Gordian knots. When we were kids, Heidi told me she had read them all. She sat down with them as if they were magazines.

"I always liked this room," I said. A bed took the place of the desk. Tito's office felt suddenly airless. "I'm really sorry I didn't go to the funeral."

## Chapter 6

"You were in the hospital," Heidi said. "You couldn't have gone. It's a locked unit."

I sat on the bed where the desk had been and missed it. The room was smaller than I thought. The living room was filled with poky furniture on painted legs, so Heidi and I used to play in the office. Tita May stacked her books on the kitchen table, and Tito had his office. The room, with its smell like incense, had been right for some games.

"Do you remember where the front lines were?" Heidi said. She toed a crooked line next to the bed. "I don't know where his desk went. We can't play Revolution without the tank."

The desk had a small cabinet in its base that a head could pop out of. Heidi wore her bike helmet for extra realism. I remembered her small fist punching open the cabinet doors. It banged every time, and she rubbed her hurt knuckles sorrowfully. I preferred to march, kneel, and throw flowers. I guess we liked the risk and the twist, that the apparent danger was after all our neighbors coming in peace, that our mothers stood their ground all the way to birthing and bringing us to the United States.

"You'd make so many signs," Heidi said. I remembered stealing Tita May's yellow legal pads. The color matched. "You used to hide them in the encyclopedias after. I'm the only one who reads them. They might still be in there."

If they were, they would be in the 2001 edition, which was marbleized red with fig leaves. Heidi had been eight, and I was ten, fifteen years after the revolution. I imagined opening a volume to an intensely scrawled sign on torn paper: PEOPLE POWER.

Heidi and I set down trivets made of woody straw before Tita May covered them with pots. Heidi put spoons next to our plates. The tray of *ukoy*, shrimp fritters, stirred something submerged in me. I didn't recognize what else there was, but the table was stuffed, barely room for my hands.

"I made your most favorite, Martha," Tita May said. "You need to eat more. You live here now. Don't worry, I won't tell your mom."

I ate a fritter: woven, woody straw.

"We're going to talk," Tita May said. "I can't trust what your mom tells me. What happened in Madison?" She asked with the quickness of family.

"The school is really big," I said. Sometimes I rode the bus to the end of the line because I didn't want to get out. I sat by the door for the stings of entering air. The driver pushed me out, and I hardly moved waiting for the next one.

"Do you know what, Martha? Don't give it one more thought," Tita May said. She piled my plate. "Stanford is the best anyway. You'll return in the fall. The time will fly by. Erning will go, too, in another year." Heidi accepted her childhood nickname from her mother, which neither of us could pronounce like she did.

I would be Heidi's shadow person. I would carry around cardboard books with candles and torn paper in their hollows. "Sounds good," I said.

"We always love you here," Tita May said. She put down her spoon. "You'll get better."

I spat food onto the side of my plate. I had passed it over in my mouth until it felt like a clean tooth.

"As for me," Tita May said, "I don't know what you heard. I didn't get to the hospital fast enough. I never saw your *tito* before he passed. Only after. Can you imagine? Fortunately, my daughter is a good girl." Heidi would punch out of the cabinet now and rub her knuckles.

"Ma, what did you do with Dad's desk?" Heidi said. Her voice had pointy edges. Her parents' names whetted on that

## Chapter 6

voice until they compacted into tough chips.

"I didn't do anything with it," Tita May said. "It's in the garage. I moved it to make space for the bed."

Heidi thought of the desk, which had been as large and unexplainable as a monolith to us, absorbing exhaust from the cars and smoke from her mother's cigarettes. "I don't think we ever told you," Heidi said. I thought of how to interrupt her.

As children, we felt a secret around the game. We kept many secrets from our mothers because we knew nothing good could come out of sharing. More history would make the game less exciting. They didn't think we were old enough for history anyway. Maybe they wouldn't let us play, either. The real revolution already belonged to our parents, and we wanted a childish version for ourselves. We didn't have many stories of our own. Even at that age, we could tell it was a story worth stealing. With a child's intuition, we knew it was a selfish game, so we didn't tell anyone.

"Martha and I used to play with Dad's desk," Heidi said. "We named the game Revolution." I frowned at my name. Tita May's face went loose, like someone had let go of the tensile strings inside. Tito was dead, so she would have to tell the stories alone.

"If you look at the desk, it's scratched from when I would come out of the tank," Heidi said. "It was one of our favorite games. I wish you wouldn't move his stuff. Why did you have to touch his desk?" I felt sorry for Heidi, who broke our young secret for this older pain.

"How old were you?" Tita May said.

"I was ten," I said. I had been too old.

"Your mom was in medical school. I was fifteen at the time," Tita May began. "I made your mom sandwiches and for the soldiers. I met your *tito* that night. Lolo Junjun introduced us. I already told you I was at the front with him."

My mother had told us how it ended, in linked arms and singing. I imagined a sky full of rockets with tails of yellow ribbons, themselves linked. My mother had been the one to start off our mania for revolution, which we kept hidden since we didn't want to complicate our game. We didn't ask for more stories, and, with time, our parents stopped talking about the revolution. When I was very young, I asked my parents whether it had been worth it, leaving their family and friends for the United States. I knew not to ask if the revolution had been worth it.

"I didn't know about this game," Tita May said. "It must have been a quiet revolution. Not ours."

With each edition, we opened volumes E and P. The encyclopedia entry on the revolution was short every year. We couldn't tie up the landline, and, even if we were allowed, the internet was too slow for our curiosity. It was faster for me to go to the past to see about our game. My mother had been right about everything. I brought back songs for us. I showed Heidi her part, how to reach for my hand after she opened the cabinet. I gave her a sandwich. Since we were shorthanded, Heidi also played the part of the radio. "Go to EDSA," she whispered. "Go now!" The door opened, and I stuffed the signs into the books.

# Chapter 7

I thought my laptop split from the fall, but it had only come unhinged. I kept crouching, enjoying the resilience at the balls of my feet as they squashed. It was interesting to use a computer while holding its halves separately. I wore headphones, so Tina would think I cracked up at the TV, but I was reading back-and-forth emails with my professor. We would produce a game show called Family Freud. Looking at the clock, I had been reading the same email for three hours. Sometimes my eyes got stuck, like a vinyl record dipping off its groove, but I popped them back in. Who would be the families? Would my dad show up for once? Tina checked on me, but I said the movie had gone tragic. I wiped my eyes. Former friends emailed that they enjoyed the dystopian mythology I sent. It was a good sign that people I barely knew liked the concept. I worked on a cladogram to show how, in an arms race, birds were evolved backwards into dragons. From there, everything was easy. The clock advanced two hours. I thought I had traveled forward, and I groaned. I forgot to do all my plans before rehearsal. Tina was trying to make a good impression on Victor as we walked over, but I was too sorrowed to help.

"What kind of name is 'Voices of Reason?'" Victor said.

"I didn't make it up," Tina said. "Nobody listens to us anyway. I really want that to change, though. The fall show is our big chance."

Unfortunately for us, Victor extended his same unimpressed nostalgia for our choir. For the week he lived with us, he observed our Tuesday night rehearsal. He never asked for the rest of our schedule. He didn't think Tina could sing like Etta James—he told us nobody can. After Victor pointed it out, the song rang spiritless to me. We were overstepping our experience, and I wasn't bold enough to push ahead. Tina kept bearing down, and her solo became too labored to sound relieved, or whatever feeling it was to find a love. She would have done better to mediate her voice with her flute, whose bloodlessness somehow gave it more soul. Tina planned to wear a sparkly top for the show, and I scowled to think of her presumptuousness. I told Marsha the show was a waste of time.

I couldn't tell Marsha the real problem, that I could feel my brain pumping out of its braincase, swelling the tiled bones until the whole thing throbbed as a second heart. I slapped my face sometimes, hoping the shock would joggle the loose bits back into order. I breathed until my stomach became a heart, too. I listened to sad music to slow myself down. Fun music was too irresistible. The most morose tracks concealed dance beats in the background until I had to obey. I clenched and loosed my hands. The knuckles shuddered from punching somebody in the face out of delight. It was a phantom hurt from high school, brought on by the coming rain. My teachers asked my mother if I was on drugs. I said anything was possible. When I got home, my mother had ripped up my mattress, and I slept on the couch. She taped up my bed, but I felt through the sheets, distinct as a pea, the scars.

## Chapter 7

Marsha said I couldn't perform if I didn't rehearse. She would give the solo to Kara.

"Kara!" I fell to my knees.

"Believe me, I don't want to," Marsha said. "That's why you have to show up."

I nodded, and all the lobes I had in me vibrated in agreement. When Tina and Victor were gone, I pushed furniture around, so I could sprint the straightest line. I tried to paint it all out, and the paint muddied my blood. Nothing could go terribly wrong if I stayed in my room. The thought of leaving, and all the flames that would streak after every color, revved me up too much. In the end, I bound myself to my bed, so I wouldn't embarrass myself.

Lying in bed wasn't any kind of bottom for me. It was almost as near to my character as happiness was. The problem was weight. Events depended on other events, and people depended on other people. If I looked at it all at once, it became a huge net with crossings so dense that the ropes were made of anvils. I lay at the bottom. As long as I lay at the bottom of the net, it held me like a hammock. If I moved, the whole thing would fly off the trees and trap me. The important thing was lying very still. The horrible thing was it was a kind of trap anyway.

"Are you okay, Martha?" Victor said. I lay in bed willing my mind gone. It was annoying to be found out, but he'd repeat himself louder if I didn't answer.

"I'm burning out," I said. I pronounced each syllable to keep the beat. "I need to relax."

"You're wearing yourself down," Victor said. "The pace in college is crazy, especially with the quarter system. You have to get used to resting when you can. Sometimes I'd stay up all night for I don't know how long and then sleep for days. It's an extreme culture."

I didn't begrudge his advice; it was true. He could have been more specific. I told him my problems.

"Time travel? Damn, Martha. Is that how you got into Stanford?" Victor said. His soft smile made me laugh. The noise echoed.

Under the covers, I didn't have many real-time distractions to ground me, so it was easy to get jammed into a loop with the past. I didn't have much control with time travel to begin with, and these loops were especially disorienting. Sometimes I saw overtly sad times, but more often the loops reached back to the previous days or the same day. I heard the same voice and same words, or saw the same thing or face, over and over again until it became meaningless and then until it became unbearable. The threshold for meaninglessness took a couple loops. I'm an impatient person. It became unbearable when I stopped feeling infuriated at the meaninglessness. The same moment happened in the same way until the end of the world. Seeing the moment again, I felt like I had picked over the bones of my life and found they had crumbled into crunchy dust.

It was morning whether the lights came from inside or outside. One morning, I noticed a new resonance in the busy sounds that passed through the vellum. The blind time in bed had sharpened my hearing. Each noise had a shadow noise at its tail, so I knew it was Victor and Tina. But the sounds had too much purpose.

"Where are you going?" I said.

I thought the world had carried on its own loop while I was under the covers, but I woke up to a new order of things.

"I'm leaving," Victor said. "I'm going back tonight. If you're feeling up to it, I'd like to take you guys to a jazz show in the city. As thanks for hosting me."

His measured, dry thanks made me suspicious. He talked

like it had been a miscalculation of hospitality, like we weren't friends.

"I know I stayed longer than I was supposed to," Victor said. "I really appreciate that you let me stay. I'll see how the auditions went. Maybe we'll all be in the Bay Area."

"I liked having you here," I said.

"I told you, Martha doesn't mind," Tina said. "I don't see why you have to go back yet. Go to the rest of your auditions at least."

"You guys need your room back," Victor said. "It's not big enough for three people."

Nobody asked whether I was free that night, and I didn't ask myself. We assumed that if I could forgo life to lie around, then I could forgo lying around for the show. I hadn't been able to forgo lying around for Victor. I hugged the guilt less closely, so I could leave bed. But I deserved it. I wasn't a good person, either.

"I don't know if I should bring you food all the time," Tina said. "If it was up to me, I would, but I don't think it's helping you."

I copied her silent eating. The feeling felt like forgetting. I had already mislaid her in my mind. I'd be lighter after she left. Friends fall away for any good reason.

"I have been trying," I said.

"I know," Tina said. "We've all been trying."

The drops of life in me gathered together like mercury. I broke a thermometer once, and the mercury came out. The metal stones had looked strong enough to sit on, but they slipped into flow under my finger. I needed to be alive for the show. I spent all day marshaling all the drops like I was a colonel in a war room. I sat in bed. I got out of bed. I was consolidating the troops. My blood was mercury. It was enough to run on. It filled the empty veins, but it slipped away. Isn't mercury poisonous? It would be my last stand.

I wanted a nice memory for our final night. I pulled together my mercury veins and brought down the knife, like they were a bunch of herbs. The mercury spilled out everywhere.

"I looked at pictures of the venue," I said. "One of those old theaters with a marquee, but the lights don't work. It's not in great shape, but who cares? Keep old theaters raw like they are. It's the way of history."

Tina drew her eyebrows and then eyes. I had consumed everything I could find about the show; I was ready. People protested for the rights of theaters. I wondered where I could get a picket sign.

"Wait long enough, and somebody breaks it," I said. "Wait longer, and somebody likes it. One man's past is another man's future. Same with jazz."

Tina curled her hair.

"Makes you think. Something's on its way," I said. "Who's coming for the movie theaters? Are we going to keep them around after they fall?"

Tina puffed out her lower lip that she filled in with red. Her face was lovely with shadows.

"They already put in fancy screens sometimes," she said.

"You're right," I said. I grabbed at her comment and pulled hard. "I'm talking about afterwards. They'd have to clear out the flippy chairs, switch out the lighting. Tear out the carpet walls. Break down the stairs. I guess it'll be a giant box. You can do anything with a box."

"They're going to tear them down. It's not the same as the old theaters. They're not pretty."

The theater could have been preserved better. Its ribs showed through the walls. A cupola on the ceiling suggested a chapel, but peeling paint made it a cave mouth. I reached

## CHAPTER 7

into a hole in the wall and would have torn out a piece of guts.

"You'll never hear this sound again," Victor said. "It's all improvised tonight." He raised his hand in an invisible toast. Tina met his toast with her bottle, and I heard the twinkle.

"Thank you for doing all this, Victor," I said. "It means a lot."

Victor's face in the dim light could have been forgiving. "I had a great time," he said.

We drifted forward to fill gaps of leaving couples. I didn't know where they went. Everyone watched the bass, guitar, and drums sit. Spotlights cast faces onto them. A roadie lady crouched and struck chords meant to tune the instruments, which we heard eagerly as if the jazz had begun.

Sometimes the jazz wasn't far away from the tuning. The musicians dressed in velvet. The bassist picked out couplets that repeated and then broke the couplets. The sound scattered before the previous sound finished. The guitarist ranged along. He shook his hair to the beat; it jumped and fell in sheets. He hit a melody that I wished would stay, but the guitar didn't dwell.

Victor and Tina figured out how to dance to the music. They shook their hair and clapped without rhythm. They filled the theater like they had filled our room. I stopped trying to follow the music. Held loosely, it ran.

I don't know how long it lasted when the music slowed. The instruments sang with a human sadness. Everyone in the theater shared the mourning and thought of themselves. The guitarist, who had been scatting with his riffs, stilled his hair and leaned into the mic.

"Woo-bee woo," he sang.

The chords sank again. The theater went blue. It was the best show I ever saw.

After Victor left, I wondered whether it made sense to get better. Getting better would prove that he was right to leave us to ourselves. I wanted to think that he could have stayed. In the end, getting better wasn't up to me. The veil cleared. Motion returned. The loops to the past settled, and watching them became boring.

Tina and I fell back into our old routine. "How'd your paper go? How's your cousin?" she'd ask. I couldn't tell if it was a regression or a restoration of whatever we had. Sometimes I thought I caught a special concern in her usual attentions. She smiled at me more or relaxed. Other times I felt that we weren't enough on our own.

Most of our time wasn't alone because the fall show approached. In high school, I sang in a choir with my mother's Filipino friends. I liked the sound of Tagalog from my voice, which I didn't hear otherwise. We performed for other Filipinos at Christmas, which made for a happy crowd and choir. At rehearsals, Tina and I girded ourselves. We both had solos, which I felt made us especially vulnerable as a powerhouse duo. I imagined the buzz in our dorm recreated all over campus. I wilted thinking of the scrutiny.

Midterms added extra frenzy. I chose a class about a man and words I didn't understand because I liked feeling disoriented. The lectures were a lot of fun, particularly the throaty German terms that sounded as unintelligible as English. Both languages had many italics, and the voice in my head read them as sly whispering. Our first paper ended the fun. Alone with the words, I realized I only understood a handful of sentences. Fortunately, these sentences took nine pages to explain.

Even Tina was cracking. "Why do I want to be a doctor again?" She laughed feebly. I had to assure Tina that I had seen her name on an envelope in the future as Dr. Valentina

## Chapter 7

Robinson. She assumed that her title was as a medical doctor and was comforted. Around this time, Tina started getting mixed up between jokes and misfortunes. She came back from organic chemistry lab one night. "Then my lab partner hides the phthalic acid from everybody, so they can't finish their experiments!" Her voice went breathy. She chuckled to herself and settled into the books on her desk.

The upperclassmen in Voices of Reason weren't immune, except for Marsha. Everyone else's hair looked showered, but the sheen came from unwashed oils. I didn't have time to sleep, but I felt relieved I had recovered enough to sing "Feeling Good" with believability. It was a rotten trick that Tina had to sing "At Last" before her organic chemistry final. The stage didn't have a curtain, so there was no minute before it opened to breathe. My breath caught.

No matter how hard I wish, I can't get away from the moment of performance. The spotlights slant out of cannons. The audience hears the beat, but I feel vibrations rising from behind. The voices lift, and the minute unmoors if I can't. I never know the person I'll be at the cue. I'd rather look into the sun than faces, sing blind than for people I don't like. I wish I won't know myself at the cue. If I could, I'd precipitate into my best, my most living substance. The lights would shake all the sickness out of me, leaving winks and flashes. Everyone would love my remains. I leaned into the mic.

"Woo-bee woo," I sang. I wasn't sure if I got the tune.

The rest of the songs passed. We all wore our best outfits and universally showered. I joined the procession out as we finished. Marsha waited for me at the foot of the stage. People still clapped, and she stuck to the darkness. I didn't notice her until her face nearly crushed into mine. I couldn't tell whose face was sweatier.

"What the hell are you doing?" Marsha said. Her eyes

seemed to sweat; they watered.

"The soul of jazz is improvisation, and we never improvise," I said.

"I understand. But couldn't you have practiced first? At least?" We pottered along to her yells until we bumped up into a corner.

"I'm sorry if I threw everyone off." I thought the group had harmonized well, but maybe their singing had been feedback from the mic. It sounded very experimental.

"My choir isn't a one-man band," Marsha said. I thought of a man with a drum strapped to his gut and laughed. "If you have creative ideas, you need to bring it up at rehearsal. We need to be honest with each other."

I have never valued honesty much. The hospital taught us that thoughts can be taken up or put down. Since then, what happened to its exactness hasn't interested me. Events have lost their hot corners and become lightweight to carry. Time travel is less interesting for this fact.

"You can't shock me into being the star. You can't sneak in a solo," Marsha said.

I didn't care about honesty, but I always had a real concern for sneakiness. The nurses in the hospital had been sneaky. They built their own whisper circle out of the walls. They knocked on the door when it was already open. The knocks had no point, other than as a warning.

Kara joined Marsha and me, her eyes wide with horror.

"Whatever you sang, it was so surreal," Kara said. "It was almost like a nightmare."

I couldn't hear what she said over the applause. No one was clapping, but my ears roared when I saw Dan.

I could have spent more time looking for Dan, but I figured that he was a necessary and immovable stake. Too much depended on our meeting for the universe to work

## Chapter 7

through a single nexus. Sometime we could be compelled together, like wind currents caught in a private tailspin. In the end, when I saw how I almost missed him, I was furious.

"It was a great song," Dan said. He was exactly the same: as lean, as mop-haired. His eyes were gray in these lights and would be green in others. I wondered how I could have ignored him in the audience, why the voltaic nerve that connected us now didn't find us much earlier.

For a long time, I wondered how I'd feel when we met. It was a rending in my chest, heavy and strange as a meteor. I realized how tired I had been all my life and shook it away. His eyes were ignition, and I read our happiness in them.

# Chapter 8

People forget traveling anywhere needs a specific destination. Since I had no idea where I would end up, the future was as unknowable as dark matter. That is, maybe dimly knowable, if I searched until I died. A million antecedents needed to be filled in before I could guess where I would end up. I didn't know where a Philosophy degree could take me, or if I would finish freshman year. Now and then, I thought I had a clue to catch up to my future self, like a conversation after class. "Have you thought about medical ethics?" a professor asked. "So many interesting problems of self-determination."

I furiously researched programs that evening. Maybe I would be in Chicago. Or Switzerland.

I have been a spatially unaware person as long as I can remember, exiting class and walking the wrong way around the Quad. Getting lost in the future would be worse than getting on the wrong bus: the wasted fare and shame of conspicuously getting out a block later. Like too many people, I wholly rely on maps in my phone, and the maps would be outdated in the future. My phone would probably be useless anyway. Philosophy classes had taught me to trust nothing.

Sometimes I felt I was made of the wrong stuff for time travel. Tina could be decisive and brave. Dan was kind. If I

## Chapter 8

wasn't so nervous, I could make something interesting out of my ability, but it was enough for me to get through the day. The breakdown bled out the boldness I had.

College kept us incoherently busy at times and in supine recovery other times. I didn't have time to search for my future self like I used to. Besides, my times in the hospital had sated my interest for a while. In the hospital, when I wasn't deathly bored with my life, I walked the eleven steps to circle my room over and over. I sat at the cinder-block desk and wrote letters. I wrote apologies and promises. My mouth talked out in therapy group like it was originating a language. In between activities, when I had nothing to do because I had already showered, I lay in bed and looked for myself. I had nothing in the hospital besides time. I could search until I died.

I hoped I would find myself at college, maybe even Stanford where I had started, but it was an old dream, and now I wanted any glimpse of my older body. I wanted to know that I would be alive later, that I would keep my promises.

The day would have a gold star next to it. My group attendance and apology for ripping a soap dispenser off the wall had earned me new privileges. I could eat downstairs in the cafeteria, which I heard had a soda machine. I could go outdoors to the psychiatric garden. The outdoors group left every morning and sometimes on request, depending on the staff person and our charms. Other patients, upset that they couldn't go outside, cried and heaved. They skipped afternoon groups, which, I reflected sadly, would hinder their chances of getting outdoors privileges.

Arrangements had been made for our psychiatric group to eat in the hospital cafeteria alone. Empty, the room was as large as my middle school gym and as foreboding, since I had been an uncoordinated child. I couldn't stop smiling when I saw the food. At least three choices were offered, and I would have called it a buffet even if I had been well. The psychiatric garden was even better. It was contained in an open square in the center of the hospital complex, enclosed by walls and one door. It was more like a park than a garden because it had two benches and a trellis. The four of us patients had the same idea and stretched in the sun.

I lay in bed at the end of the day. The nurses' station was positioned outside my door, and they had stopped talking about me. I didn't have to sleep with a pillow pushed into my ears, which had been giving me a headache. Emboldened by comfort, good food, and nature, I decided to look for myself at Stanford. If I continued to progress at the rate I had today, I could get back to college. Thank God I didn't go through with exploding that soap dispenser yesterday!

Everybody thinks the Quad is the best part of campus, so I traveled and sat for a beat. During my first round at Stanford, I dragged my feet around, unable to shake the horror that I had fallen into the wrong lane in a pinball machine. The flippers couldn't reach me, and I was stuck by a trick of the game. Now, coming from the hospital, the Quad was many times larger than the cafeteria, a cathedral without a roof. It reminded me of the psychiatric garden since it was square and surrounded by walls, but these walls had many open doors.

I stood by the statues. I flipped around days and weeks, at first diligently and then feverishly when my concentration curled and frayed. In high school, I watched a friend run a race. I waited near the finish line, trying to focus on all the runners and then individual runners to find my friend. I didn't know what he was wearing. Flipping through time in the Quad felt the same, and the lack of seasons made the challenge more disorienting. The search had taken on com-

## Chapter 8

pulsion, and the longer I looked, the longer I needed to look.

Same as the present, other people passed me in streaks of public color, while I watched from the only slow pocket. I wondered whether all their clockwork routines made something more than movement. When somebody slipped out of activity, I caught myself looking for her instead of me. Seen at double time from a distance, other people's lives could have been mine.

I stopped for the dress: watercolor blue and cream in a pattern of lilies or fire. My mother and I had gone to a department store after church. I grabbed it off the rack with a tingle of premonition. The cloth smelled like a grown-up child, all freedom and freshness in a flowery musk. A lawyer in a movie we liked wore sleeveless pastel dresses. On my body, the dress floated against my skin, like the great life I would wear lightly someday. If I squinted, the pattern matched my glasses. I found the dress on the same day as the dance, which felt like a triumph. I had a good time dancing that night, and I thought the future would be full of tests like choosing dresses.

Dan was with me. He was exactly the same. The dress still fit. It fanned from my hips when we biked across the Quad, a messenger bag hitting my thighs metronomically. I saw the movie lawyer walk past offices and fountains. I recognized the dress before I recognized my face, which was browner and nicer than the pallid chicken skin I caught in the mirror now and then. I tried not to look in mirrors these days, so my face would have been a shock even if it wasn't prettier than it had any right to be. I looked for some marker of the fake faces that followed me around the hospital, but I knew by its roughness that the body couldn't be a plant. It was mine.

Maybe I never believed in fate. I had seen everything I

wanted. The hospital room was still and anonymous. The beige and sage curtains were carefully inoffensive. It was too much, from here to there, and the interval snapped like a busted bridge. In the mirror, I tried to smile, and the eyes were afraid of myself. It was enough to make me spit.

The light in the room grew from a line. Somebody had come in without knocking. I rolled over to face the visitor: a circle-eyed woman pushing a metal cart. She extracted a clipboard from her cart.

"Music?" she asked. "You can check one out." The Walkman was halfway from her hands into mine. The pencil slipped in my fingers as I signed my name into her list. She passed me a padded binder of CDs. I watched the prisms from the disk. I wondered the pressure it would take to crack it along its rainbow.

"You return it when you leave," the woman told me. She noted *Songs Without Words* next to my name.

The next morning, I keyed up my Walkman. There would be twenty-five songs. I closed my eyes and stretched in the sun.

# Chapter 9

Dan and I went home. I thought Dan looked exactly my type, but I didn't have much choice where I grew up, so I couldn't be sure. I knew I was more attracted to blond hair than brown. I hardly felt sexual, so I clung to the vague stirrings because they seemed the right shape. After first sight faded, I waited for the starved feeling to return, the wolfish urge to start our life together. But, alone in my room after the show, Dan smiled contentedly. The belonging gave me relief, not the delirium I was supposed to feel for my future husband. I wondered if I was bored because I already knew the end of the story. He acted like he knew, too.

"If we get married, our grandparents will sit down at our wedding," he said in bed. He caressed my hair. "What do you think they'll talk about? I bet they never thought they'd have Polish-Filipino-American great-grand-kids."

Things were moving too fast. I guess I wasn't used to hearing the future from another person, or maybe I wasn't as romantic as I thought. It was enough to make me rethink our marriage, until we went up the mountains.

It would be our first date. Dan convinced Tina to lend her car, so I knew his surprise had to be a good idea. He wouldn't slow down, and the car climbed into fog that tore and reformed around us. The elevating air thinned and condensed. The breathlessness was everything I was supposed to feel. I hadn't seen this ending yet.

This horizon, near to the sky as we were, hardly changed size as we approached. Cities from a distance zoom from toys into monsters. The trees stayed put. We shrank when we walked at their roots. The smell of soil and age mingled in the air, among the particles that swam like starlight. I'd never see the treetops. I gave up and decided to live in the moss, where the great lines of the redwoods began. I looked at Dan, his face greened in the shade, and I knew we'd be together forever.

"How did you know?" I said.

"I love redwoods. It's one of my favorite places."

I grabbed for his hand.

"I thought it'd be a surprise," Dan said. "But I'm glad you like it here. I didn't know you've been here already."

"I don't know if I have."

Maybe it was the time travel, but sometimes I've recognized myself in new places. The recognition is more real than the place itself, impenetrable as a wall or a dream. Things get transparent in this moment.

The ancient trees got us feeling like we were running out of time. Our conversations finally had the urgency that they were supposed to. I felt like we couldn't talk fast enough to know each other. We were already losing the moment the longer we talked. We wanted to kill it and live in it until we died, at the same time. The beginning was too precious to keep, too fine to free. We had to tell each other everything before the trees ran out. It was nonsense, but we didn't have anything bigger to say yet.

"I'm the luckiest man in the world, to be with you," Dan said. I agreed.

## Chapter 9

"You're something special, Martha," Dan said. "I've never met a girl like you before. You could change history if you wanted to."

I had already explained to Dan that he could go places I couldn't, even with the time travel. Most of the events he wanted to see were driven by people who looked like him, and I'd get in trouble if I tried to mess around. I listened to our feet break the dirt.

"I'd give anything for your talent, to travel in time. I didn't tell you yet, but I wanted to study history before. In high school, I got interested in World War Two. It was an obsession," Dan said. In this mood, we offered up our short lives like they were epics.

"I read all the biographies I could find. That's how I got interested in psychology," he said. "History is made by crazy people."

I wanted to tell Dan that I didn't make things; I broke them.

For years, I wondered what would have happened if I told him everything right then, the illness that exploded my life into magics. People think time travel is an adventure, but they look at me strangely when I talk about my adventures in madness. Besides, the redwoods grove wasn't any place to tell Dan. I'd tell him who I was, the lake and afterwards, when we found the right place. Or maybe I wouldn't say anything at all, so he could see for himself. Then he could tell me what he saw.

Dan and I stamped down earth that sprang up again as soon as we left it. I reached for something insightful to say, but I didn't have anything. Dan had enough insight for us both.

"Think about any war. It comes down to a battle between who's crazier. Some guy or the other guy," Dan said. He picked over rocks while we walked. "History is decided by one crazy guy who wins. When I'm a psychologist, I'll change history by helping people. Who knows what happens to the world if you change one person?"

I didn't follow, but anything sounded impressive in this leafy light. A lot of freshmen talked like him, about saving and inventing things. I hoped I would soon. Anyway, at the start, a person can't know sincerity from delusion in a lover. He can't know, either.

"Do you really think it comes down to one guy? What about revolution?" I said.

"You're right, sometimes it's more people. But do you think revolutionaries are sane?"

People say the trees make poets out of people, and I grabbed at the poetry I knew. Nobody could say poets were sane. I didn't have any moment that could stand up next to these trees. My mother did, and I told her story as if it was my own. I had practiced enough. The air became sacred, like it always did when I tried to say the vastness of her life. Maybe I had practiced too much. The story was all corners and facts. The best parts of my life belonged to other people.

"Everyone I know went to EDSA," I said. "I've heard the stories a million times. They all showed up, my mom showed up, and they overthrew one crazy guy. They won. I can't believe you never heard about the revolution, Dan. It was a big deal. You said you liked history. Are you sure you didn't forget?"

The trees filtered the wind into sighs. The trees unrolled into their circles, the years they held. I listened. Dan told me how his parents won. He understood where I lived, in the space after the revolution, and I wanted us to stay in our common country. It was a story big enough for our love and the trees.

## Chapter 9

I hoped he wouldn't laugh, like I sometimes had to, that our lives were the let-down after somebody else's climax. Our hike in the trees became a march, to our parents' metronome.

"Did the revolution make a difference?" Dan asked.

I could say anything I wanted. They won so that we could tell the stories. I weighed, but I couldn't see. And even if I traveled in time, one crazy girl can't overthrow that kind of history, their power. I only had one picture, the story I was given. He asked me the question I had been too afraid to ask my parents, whether the revolution was worth it. I grew up thinking I'd answer with my life, make it worth it, so my parents wouldn't have to wonder. But now I was grown, and I couldn't even stay alive without going mad.

"I don't know," I said.

I had no answer, saw only the faces of heroes that he didn't know. I'd tell him their faces if I could, but I had never known them, either. My best memories weren't real; I wanted them anyway. I wanted to shake Dan out of his calculations, his historian's counterweights and figures. It wasn't the historian's job to judge.

In another age, our Marcelo-Mazursky child would claim three countries and one story. She would visit the skeletons of her countries in World War Two and see where her people came from. Buildings shot to bones, windows blown out to black eyes. She would open the encyclopedias and read, in the crowded revolution, where her parents were born and her grandparents grew old.

I couldn't tell where the sun was coming from, but the grooves in each trunk collected gold like rainfall. We would meet the end of the trees soon, and I turned us around. I didn't want to see the gold become grass.

"Do you think people got used to it, living around these redwoods?" Dan said. The way back was faster.

"A person can get used to anything," I said. We were walking too quickly. "Do you think these trees will be here forever?" I knew without asking what kind of man my husband was, but I needed to check.

"I don't know. The Allies thought the Ardennes Forest was impenetrable. But the tanks plowed them down, like every other place. It's awful, what they did to the trees."

# Chapter 10

Waking up in Tito's office among his old things felt like a fresh start. The shelves of encyclopedias insulated the room, so it stayed warm throughout the Bay Area winter. Tita May said it was the warmest spot in the house. The three of us sat around in the evenings and continued the talk from dinner. Tita May usually took up cake or a crunchy snack. The books had a soundproofing effect, so sounds from the street reached us as muffled noise. It made me feel like we were the only people left in the world.

Looking back on those months I lived with Tita May and Heidi, I don't know how they spent time with me. After a few days, I wanted to reciprocate their kindness by showering. At home, I thought that my body didn't make a difference without my mind. At first, being dirty felt like liberation, the only choice I still had. I'd lose this choice, too. It was different when I lived with Tita May and Heidi. Something like self-pride had started in me again because I wished I had things to say. They had the same filmy veil around them like everyone else, but I knew they were real.

My vision worked fine, as far as I could tell, except for books. When I was well, I didn't need to think about words or their shapes. The shapes of words said things to me automatically. When I was sick, the shapes of words got silent. The shapes slid around on paper. I had to check the shapes against my memory of the word. Then I had to check the word against my memory of my life, which was harder than remembering how to read. I started getting interested in stories again, though, and Heidi read to me when she got home.

Heidi came home from lab at the same time on weekdays, but the rumble of the garage door opening shocked me every time. I don't clearly remember what I did before she got home. No matter what I was doing, the noises she made filled me with discomfort I couldn't name. I would call its closest emotion guilt. The sequence of aural anticipation didn't change: garage door rumbling, car door shutting, trunk shutting, keys jingling, steps to the door, and escaping air when the door opened. I knew I loved Heidi, but these homecoming noises made me sit on my hands out of dread. One day, without deciding to, I walked up to the door and opened it. The trunk was still shutting. As the trunk came down, Heidi adjusted her bags and saw me. The garage door had already rumbled shut, so the room was dark and dirty. She looked surprised and then smiled. I realized I hadn't seen her in a long time.

Heidi's favorite book is *Surely You're Joking, Mr. Feynman!* It's been her favorite book since she was ten. She tried to lend me copies, but I lost them. I thought she'd be disappointed when she became a scientist herself, but she had as much fun. She read to me nights and whenever I wanted. The words slid around, but I mostly caught them. She got to parts that made her laugh and cover her mouth sometimes, so I asked her to say those bits over until I understood. The book had a lot of bits like that, or she had the right sense of humor for it, because we spent a lot of time and hardly

## Chapter 10

got through it. Her voice with that book told me about the things that could happen if I left the house. A lot could happen. People were meeting other people and talking quickly.

On the first day she left for work, Tita May left me spare keys on the kitchen counter. Her heels clicked on the tile as she opened cabinets to show me food, how to use the oven if I wanted to cook, not to worry about dishes. The loop had two keys for the padlock and keyhole. I didn't need the keys because if I wanted to leave, I'd leave for good. I'd turn the key from the inside and wouldn't stop walking. Sometimes I planned how to run away, but I didn't get farther than how to shut the door behind me. I tired myself out thinking about all the preparations to take the keys from the counter.

Running away was my reason for coming to Tita May and Heidi. When Scott dropped me off at the airport, I felt the thud of determination that I'd been waiting for. I passed all kinds of exits and wandering-off points from airport to airport, but I kept procrastinating until the exits ran out. I thought the right spot would have a look to it. A portal with some finality, some weight. I never saw it.

I don't remember if I was taking my medications yet. In my memory, this time feels unhurried but not slow. Medicated times have a stillness to them. The doctors told me the medications would help me stay in the present. I didn't take any at first because time travel was part of myself that I got to keep. I didn't aim to go anywhere because leaving time would take as much work as leaving the house. But I didn't want to give myself up to get well.

Tita May acted like she hadn't talked to my mother. She never knew me as well as Heidi, so I thought maybe she didn't see what I had lost. Heidi, for all her love, looked at me sadly sometimes. Tita May talked to me as fast as she always did. She kept smelling my hair as usual, even before I thought to be kinder. She acted like she didn't have anything to be worried about. On my end, I wasn't sure how strange I was behaving, but I knew most people had stopped talking to me. At that time, people fell away from me for reasons I never found out. They must have been good reasons. Tita May wouldn't stop talking.

My mother would have told Tita May that I didn't go outside anymore. At the start, I hated being seen. After a few weeks, the sun didn't interest me. When I was outside, I felt like my clothes were made of paper. The wind blew through me, but I didn't feel it at all. My skin became paper, too. Manipulating its folds when I talked or moved was too much to think about. My mother says she found me standing with my back to the house, wearing the pajamas I didn't take off. The snow wet my feet. I didn't move when she touched my shoulder and led me dull-eyed into the house.

Tita May acted like she hadn't heard about all this business. She didn't know that I wasn't eating, either. She cooked the same elaborate meals, even if I sometimes missed my mouth bringing food into it. I wasn't disinterested in food, but eating would take away focus from the same thing that occupied my mind whether my eyes were open or closed. I was using my mind to get far away.

I used to visit Tita May and Heidi frequently, but I never got to where I wasn't a guest. It wasn't for a lack of trust or comfort. Tita May never completely relaxes, which I picked up on as a child and kept seeing. Movement is her original position, and she buzzes around Heidi with the same hospitality. She worked late hours and went to work in the kitchen straight after. She couldn't stop moving, so she started fixing outings for us on the weekends. I guess whatever kindness was in me kept growing because I went. The first time I had an interesting idea about these outings. The idea had

## Chapter 10

the right look to it, so I knew I should do it. I was getting very good at using my mind to get me far away. It'd be an interesting experiment to practice my powers outside.

Tita May has photos from these outings: trolleys, towers, baseball, water. I'm smiling in the photos, but it's an experimental smile. Now and then, I get a piece of what stayed in me from this time.

The trees made the woods dark. The noise was constant, crunching like bones. I couldn't see the treetops, only lines to the sky. Sun as starlight. I was as small as I knew myself to be.

"What are you thinking, Martha?" Heidi asked.

"They're too strong," I said.

# Chapter 11

Tina, misaligned from drinking after the party, bent over and held my notebook close. Her breath wasn't level, either, and came out jagged. "You're making a tree," she said.

I sat by the light of the moon, which gave a more cooperative glow than the overhead fluorescent bulbs. Books that I didn't have time to put away were thrown half-open on the floor. I'd decided there wasn't a better time to do laundry, and Tina's underwear was strung above my desk like tinsel.

"It's literally a tree and symbolically a monument," I said. "Actually, it's metal, so it can't literally be a tree. It's literally a monument and symbolically a tree. You're right!" I laughed hard. Tina laughed with me. She flopped onto my desk.

"Marsha needs to get the sticks out of her ass," Tina said. "She won't stop going on about how you ruined the show. It's all she wants to talk about."

She unfolded the map I made while she was at the party. It was a schematic of subway lines made from the roots of the tree. The Bay Area needs better public transit.

"So you think I sounded okay?" I asked. I worked as we talked, using a second canvas to wipe charcoal from my fingers for the perfect texture.

"Martha, it was terrifying," Tina said. "But who cares?

## Chapter II

It's a corny college choir. It isn't Carnegie Hall." Her updo had untangled into fuzz from the rain. "Damn," she said, fingering a braid.

"No, it isn't," I said. Heat gathered in my forehead, and I pressed my cooler hand to it. Tina picked up the small bristlecone pine that I had twisted from paper and labeled 'NO!' with a sticky note. A small brontosaurus bit empty air high above the pine's treetop, with a sad expression.

"Marsha and I have the same name, practically," I said. I kept my tone ambiguous.

"Very close," Tina agreed. "It's weird."

I could proceed. "It could get confusing," I said. I kept my eyes on my work, but I had an eye for her.

Tina frowned. "Confusing how?"

"I'm not sure." It was all I had.

"You have different last names," Tina said. "And you look totally different. You're, like, different races, Martha. Plus, you're an artist!"

She showed me my drawing of a camouflaged tank—literally a tank, symbolically a forest—bouncing off a giant gold tree. Mist swirled around. I smiled.

"Not like her pedestrian ass," Tina said. "You're completely original, Marsha!"

In the morning, Tina acted like she didn't remember our conversation, which would have been suspicious if she had been anyone else at the time. The curtains and door had to stay banged, so I squeezed into the crack between the door and hallway. I brought her a tray for lunch and sat at the foot of her bed. I tried to think if she usually waited for me to wake up or woke me up, but she opened her eyes before I remembered. She closed her eyes as I reviewed.

"It's for my fellowship application," I said. "Did you really forget? I'm interested in fortifications." I had already sealed the models in customized boxes, so I had nothing to jog her memory.

"Okay," Tina said. She drank coffee lying down, which should have been a choking hazard. Or, if she missed her mouth, she could burn herself.

"If the Ardennes Forest had been metal, it would have been truly impenetrable," I said. "It would have been a game-changer. The Allies would have won!" I let my thesis hang in the air. It wouldn't take much more effort to dig the models out of the packing peanuts.

"The Allies did win," Tina said. "If you really think it's a game-changer, why don't you go back and try it?" She shaded her eyes with her hands and stared at the ceiling.

She was a real pain when she was hungover. "Tina, I'm not trying to get myself killed!"

"What kind of fellowship is this?" She sat up slowly.

"It's the Bond-Rummy Freshman Fellowship. It's not enough for the whole project. It's for the prototype. A single tree for now."

Tina checked her hair in the mirror mournfully. "Well, they love their prototypes around here."

I stuck my best designs into a giant envelope. At the post office, I'd gotten stamps with circus seals on them. I hoped they would be proof of my sense of humor.

"Martha, you don't need a stamp. The office is down the street," Tina said. I scratched off the stamp.

"I need to start over," Tina said to her hair, throwing up her hands. She was awake now.

I stacked the boxes onto a dolly I borrowed from the residential staff. It was a flat dolly made for moving furniture. None of the boxes was big, so they occasionally fell through the gaps in the base of the dolly. By the eighth time, I rummaged through a dumpster for a large box, which I stuck

## Chapter 11

all my smaller boxes inside. The new box, full of boxes, fit perfectly. It was dirty, though, so I wiped it down.

On my way back from dropping off my application, I stopped into the counseling center. The building chuckled today: a child's drawing of a box house with a curly-smoke chimney. If I expected the universe to make good on its promises, I needed to keep my word, too. I was in a virtuous mood. Dan told me he had already used up his free counseling sessions. He liked to observe their methods. He said they had good methods. I had been meaning to see if I could roll over my sessions to him.

The waiting room had too many cracks for people to conceal themselves. I sat in a couch-chair as stiff as a chair in the skin of a couch. I heard people rustling around and ripping magazine pages, but they sat in other alcoves. I guessed the isolation was for our own confidentiality. For similar reasons, the doctors didn't say our names when they came in. They stared expectantly and meaningfully at us until we remembered we needed them.

I remembered Dr. Walsh immediately. She was still around my age. We had kept apace in the last year. With her white hair liberated from its braids, it fell in crimps. It looked much better. She had earned a true identification badge now, and its microchip winked at me.

"I'm Dr. Walsh," the shadow person said. The shadows left when she spoke. Her business card said the counseling center was her fellowship, so I guessed she had graduated school since our last meeting. At least one of us had followed through.

"Right," I said. "I know." I understood she wasn't allowed to acknowledge me for confidentiality, so I stared at her expectantly and meaningfully. Behind her, a painting of a sea roiled.

"It's your first time at the counseling center," Dr. Walsh said. She knew a lot of words. She should have said more words before. Her supervisor had been too cruel, I suppose.

"My boyfriend had a good experience," I said. "He strongly recommended it. I trust him because, firstly, he is my future husband. Secondly, he is studying the same things you did, Dr. Walsh."

Dr. Walsh smiled and nodded. "You wanted to see for yourself."

She was as nice as I remembered. It felt gauche to bring up rollover options, given our prior relationship.

"If it's okay with you, I have a few questions to ask before we begin," Dr. Walsh said. She scanned her clipboard. "You don't need to answer if you're uncomfortable. Let me know. How old are you?"

"I'm old for my year." Sometimes the gap year was something visible I needed to explain. "Third time's the charm. Like in my life." She didn't laugh. She wasn't nice anymore.

"Where are you from?" Dr. Walsh asked.

"My family is from the Philippines, but I grew up in Wisconsin." I yawned. Dr. Walsh checked a box. I apologized. "What about you, where are you from?"

"I'm from Wisconsin. What's a day in your life?"

"What?" I thought. Tubes tipped with mushrooms were coming out of the ceiling. I shivered.

"Is the vent bothering you? They crank up the air conditioner," Dr. Walsh said. "It's a problem."

"Back to your question," I said. "I try to make the most of my time. Usually." She made a note. She reread her note.

"Okay, Dr. Walsh. I didn't end up finishing that therapy group," I admitted. "I quit after the first day and moved to San Jose." I rolled my eyes, alluding to the Sudoku memory restoration exercise. She blushed.

## Chapter II

"No offense," I said. "It's not like you were the one. I didn't get the point of it. What was the point?" If I found out, I could finally answer Heidi.

Dr. Walsh handed me a purple paper. "It sounds like you're interested in groups? We have several going here."

I read the acronyms on the flyer. "How old are people?"

"Other people in the group? It's open to all Stanford affiliates. Undergraduate and graduate students, some staff. It's mixed gender. I don't know if you have a preference."

I frowned.

"You can take time to think about it," Dr. Walsh said. She made her eyes outgoing. "We can go over the rest of the questions later. We'll have time later. How are you feeling today?"

"Today? I feel amazing," I said. "Honestly, I feel like I could bounce off a building. Not literally, Dr. Walsh." She had started to braid her hair in frantic twisting. I sighed.

"Actually, I can think of one way you can help me," I said. Dr. Walsh adjusted her cape.

"I have a problem, and I don't know what to do," I said.

She rounded her eyes and showed me teeth. "I'm here to listen," she said. She reminded me of Victor.

"I have too many ideas."

---

Time was streaming at its best pace. It projected ahead to pull me easily, but it was slow enough to surprise. And the surprises delighted me. I watched ants move with the synchrony of one body, tones in music surface, rare combinations of foods twirl in my stomach. At sex, I got to the frontier of invention. My voice had come back, louder and wiser, in class and with my friends. Things to say now spilled. I was keeping up with the best of them, and I would outrun them all soon. I continued to accelerate while they idled, braked, and fell to the ground. They'd get in the way of my next lap unless they got their shit together.

Scott kept up, and I hated myself for not loving him sooner. He also regretted the dead time before we discovered our connection, and he said as much in our conversations. *I wish we talked when you lived at home! But at least we're talking now*, he said in a text. My phone vibrated as if it had direct possession of his buzzing vocal chords.

*I know! I can't believe I hated you so much when you and Ally got married!* I texted in reply. I used his name for my mother, in part a concession to his right to rename and in part to minimize confusion. *Apparently, eleven years is enough time for a child to learn how to hate. You've always loved Ally, even if I didn't see it. You stuck by us during all the departures of life, including the departure of my mind.*

Scott texted back a line of crying emoticons. I counted six, which was the years in my life before he came into it. I replied with thirteen smiling emoticons, which completed my years of life, although the unlucky number unsettled me.

My mother, motivated by my bonding with Scott, got tickets to San Jose for Parents Weekend. Mentally and sometimes physically, I rehearsed what I would say to my stepfather.

"Hi, Dad. If the offer is still good to call you 'Dad.' Expiration dates are more of a suggestion anyway. And not a thing in most countries." I wanted to communicate something light yet substantial, and the humorous reference to our previous cultural friction seemed like a necessary touch.

Scott and Ally make a good-looking couple, which was another reason to hate Scott. At eleven years old, I had angry eyebrows and a mustache like my father, as well as a general mood of pretentiousness. I hoped that my lack of fit came from living among white people, but my mother slid into things with an ease that made immigration look good. She is beautiful beyond borders, and photos confirm my early memories. She has eyes like baths and hair that swishes like a sail catching wind. Her take on Filipino friendly, which I didn't stay long enough to learn, suited the Midwestern neighborliness we found ourselves in. My father's homesickness validated my lonely feelings, but I wasn't homesick for anything I knew.

My mother tells me that I loved Scott when I first met him, which she says was at church. My father didn't go to church, which made him strange among the Filipino set and, early on, an enigmatic figure for me. During the winters especially, when leaving the house in my too-small coat seemed sacrificial, I felt jealous that my father could stay home. Still, the conflict for me came with my sadness that I might not see him after we died, and, stranger still, that he didn't seem to care. At the time, I didn't know that our separation and his indifference would happen much sooner.

I do remember seeing Scott at confession a lot, about a year before he moved in with us. I don't know what he was confessing, but I always had the same sins. Whenever I walked into church, despair came over me. I couldn't remember if despair was a sin or not, but I felt guilty anyway. I couldn't focus on the priest; my soul was full of pride, which everybody said was the worst one. I only thought of myself, the whole way through, compared myself to front faces and backsides of heads. Even seen backwards, heads have a lot to tell. Past a certain shade, the front face wasn't white. It wasn't an infallible system, but I relied on it.

The first thing I did at church was count how many dark hairs I saw, choked when it wasn't enough. Even when it was enough, I felt depressed because I saw by the posture of their spines that they fit in better than me. Their clothes hung more easily. Sometimes in the bathroom, I looked at my face and dreaded what I saw, which was vanity, too. The only time I conquered pride was when I sang hymns, so I sang as loud and often as I could manage. When we weren't allowed to sing, I sang in my head. A lot of people have tics, and I sing silently a lot. In the end, moving to California was the best thing for my spiritual life.

Knowing what I do now, I really think the problem was, at bottom, everything to do with Anne of Green Gables. I read the series until some of the spines creased to white. Then I had to reread the rest until they creased along the same lines. I ended up taping the bindings when they tore. I'd wake up some mornings from being Anne's friend or living in Anne's house, and the digital clocks, cereal boxes, and cars ripped pieces out of me. We didn't have enough vales anymore. Where were all the trees? I figured out, from my excursions in time, that I couldn't have been friends with Anne. She was progressive for her century, I knew, but even Anne couldn't help the structure of things, where people were born and how they got to live. She liked books as much as I did, so she met all her friends at school. I wasn't sure I would have been allowed to go to their school. But maybe Canada was different.

I could have resisted the system, like Anne in her time, but I beat myself up instead. Years later, I learned the term for this complex in one of my philosophy classes and forgot it. It was something about self-hatred to the point of absurdity. I can't ever remember the term because Tina made up her own, which is what stuck.

"Are you having Anne of Green Gables FOMO again?" Tina said.

"No," I said. "I wish you'd stop asking."

My mother collects absurdities, and she was always laughing during our first decade in Wisconsin, especially in church. People say the transition is harder for the first generation, but she ended up explaining things to me regularly, the harmlessness of people who didn't know. She fluffed them up until their approval, which they gave generously to our cause, became funny. Unlike me, people commented that she was fitting in, that her English was great. Nobody told her that she was suspiciously quiet. I really thought it had something to do with my face, which was worse than hers. She kept her indefinable accent, a softened cadence here and there that mesmerized equally with her beauty, for the rest of her life. Her laugh was accentless.

Scott and Dan's meeting at Parents Weekend would be crucial because it showed that I accepted Scott and Ally. I texted Scott, *You and Dan will have a lot to talk about I'm sure! Haha! (He's white.)* I was glad that we could discuss race parenthetically.

"I'm sure we'll have a lot to talk about," Dan said. Breaks between classes, where I used to feel Tina's absence, weren't long enough for our time alone, since my room was a rare shield from surveillance. "I want to hear about your antisocial middle school phase."

"It wasn't a phase," I said. I winked at him. "I can't wait for you to meet my mom. She's an angel. I'd say she's got a heart of gold if gold wasn't soft. She's harder than teeth even. The non-gold kind."

Dan looked impressed. "She sounds like a really nice person."

"Harder than ivory tusks. Anyhow, you'll get to meet Heidi finally," I said. After ten days of dating, it drove me insane that he didn't know people in my life. "She's my best friend. Other than Tina and you. She's my oldest friend. She's way nicer than Tina." I giggled.

"I like Tina," Dan said. I rolled my eyes. He always had to have a cause.

"Of course I like Tina," I said. "She's my friend, not yours. But she has this indifferent quality to her. Like she's waiting for something, and you're waiting for something, and you're friends because you're standing in the same line."

Dan hummed.

"Heidi and I are different," I said. "If we were in a crowd, she'd find me. We're like that." I rolled over for more sex.

When I saw my family, we crossed the parking lot from opposite sides. Since it was Parents Weekend, visiting cars crowded the lot, side by side with the friendly cars belonging to students. Each car was labeled with blue tags or poison ones. I didn't know what the new cars had to offer, but I got a bad feeling. I made a path from the reliable cars and weaved in and out. Dan followed.

From the far end of a tunnel, my parents' approaching faces had a destined look to them. Horizon lines radiated from their heads like they were the vanishing points in a medieval painting, when perspective was invented. Heidi and Tita May completed the line. I couldn't wait and jogged a bit, deciding to hug Scott first to make up for my sins. For homeostasis, I yelled, "Mommy!"

"So good to see you, Martha," Scott said.

"Mom, this is Dan," I said. I brought Dan's hand into Scott's hand. "Dan, this is Scott, May, Heidi, Alma—oops, Ally. I mean, Mom. May and Heidi, this is Dan. Scott, this is Dan." I traded all the hands.

"Martha, calm down," Heidi whispered. I understood the voices.

Dan had a strong handshake. I saw veins pop from his wrist: tumescent worms after the rain that breaks the drought. My heart, tumescent with love, humbled itself for Heidi's

## Chapter 11

sake. She had not had one boyfriend in all her life.

"Hello there, Dan," Tita May said. She layered extra music into her voice. Her hand was heavy with bangles, but Dan's wormy wrist won.

"Oh my god, so handsome!" she whispered to me. I shushed the voices. Heidi was right there.

"On to the meat. What's for eating?" I said. "Nobody became a vegan? Believe me, it's Good Friday. It's gotta be. It feels good, doesn't it. Eat what you want! No need to be an ideologue about everything. Said Jesus." I made my face colloquial. Hospitality. Tomorrow was Saturday.

"Eat meat!" I got their attention. Everybody nodded.

"You show the way," Ally said. She kissed my head and smoothed my hair.

It was the only possible spot. I ordered the same dish at the same place most meals lately. The loco moco plate was nothing I'd tried before moving to California. "I love the Midwestern slab-of-meat homeyness and rice until oblivion," I said. Everybody nodded. What it all symbolized got me thinking about Hawaii someday. It was closer to the Philippines, and it had an island. Nobody laughed. My family and Dan absorbed my dreams and food thoughtfully.

"Psychology! Sure, sure," my mother said. "With the intention of medical school?" A fast eater, she pushed back her plate.

"No, I'm thinking clinical psychology," said Dan. "I'm passionate about mental wellness. I don't think medication should be the default treatment. I don't know, though, it could change."

He smiled shyly at me, ostensibly his inspiration and the wellness in question. I'd make up my mind later.

"That's awesome. My area is neurochemistry," Heidi said. "My dad was a psychiatrist."

Dan bowed.

"Psychiatrists are somewhat weird," Tita May said. She addressed Dan. They sat next to each other, so she couldn't face him as she talked. "My husband had a different way of looking at things. For example, he liked to iron the newspaper. Can you imagine? Easier for reading and not as dirty, he said. Crazy. He never ironed clothes."

She drank her wine, and the fringe of her eyelashes hid her eyes.

"He loved to read. The same as my uncle," Tita May went on. "Me, I never even open a book. Martha is like them."

Heidi squeezed my hand. I laid the hand to my forehead and glanced at Dan. It was all getting too weird.

Dan put his hand on Tita May's shoulder, and her same-side hand curved sideways to hold his. Claw-like. Heidi, eyes unmoving, thinned her lip.

"I have good news," said Heidi, thin-lipped, moving un-eyes. "I got into MIT."

I couldn't hear the rest over our cheering. The restaurant was empty otherwise, so we didn't hold back. It wasn't usually this empty.

"And I'm going to go," Heidi said.

Tita May, squeaky as a mouse at the bottom of a barrel, nodded.

"Oh, Heidi. Congratulations. Amazing." My mother clapped and tilted her head. She was admiring an invisible dog on the street. The dog's name was Heidi. Scott started on the first of his questions.

"More good news," I said.

Heidi's eyes widened in anticipation. She couldn't wait.

"I got the fellowship!"

The noise sounded almost equal, which seemed fair.

## Chapter 11

After dinner, we paced squares around campus, and Dan took up with Tita May. I wasn't sure if the pairing came from being leftovers from the two natural couples: Heidi and me, Scott and Ally. Heidi and I outran the others, and I looked back at Dan lifting his ears at Tita May with secret focus.

"I can't wait for Boston," Heidi said. We linked arms, which made it hard to dodge the hedges. "All the history. You can't go anywhere without bumping into old stuff. Not like California."

"MIT is in Cambridge," I said.

"Boston is across the bridge," Heidi said. "And I like Cambridge, too. It has a ton of bookstores. Central Square is really cool. It's fun to walk around."

"Cambridge is where the intellectual oligarchy sends their heirs to be trained as the liberals who will inherit the earth," I said. "Good food, though."

"What are you even talking about," Heidi said. She stopped in front of a statue sitting on a bench. "Martha, honestly, are you on crack or something?"

"What do you know about crack? And no, I'm not on anything."

"Okay, because you're being an asshole," Heidi said. Her voice cracked. "And I really need to talk to someone right now."

"You can always talk to me," I said. The words came automatically. Hearing them, I sobered.

"Mom's not doing well," Heidi said. "At all. You heard her at dinner. Telling Dan about Dad. Why does she have to talk about Dad all the time? Talking about his newspapers. She doesn't care about dumb newspapers. And now I'm leaving her for college. I'm really worried about her. She's been holding it together for years."

Tito died almost a year ago. She was talking out of order, and I tried to track it.

"I didn't think the newspapers were that weird," I said. "It was kind of a good idea actually."

"You haven't seen her like I have," Heidi insisted. "She's not herself. She doesn't cook anymore. She skips work. I came home from school, and she was sleeping in front of the TV in her underwear. The curtains were open and everything." She dropped her voice as she listed the taboos.

"She doesn't talk to me anymore," Heidi said. Her face deformed, and I tried to recognize her.

The last point worried me. When we were kids, I almost forgot what Tita May and Heidi looked like apart. They crossed rooms and people to be together as long as the other was around. Their looks harmonized, even when they weren't wearing matching clothes: Heidi a smaller, inflated version of her mother, nodding after her with a bobble head. Heidi didn't understand that sitting at the adults' table made her look like a loser. Tita May didn't see that joining the kids' table had overstepped cute eccentricity. And Heidi's gentleness reflected, in the way metal reflects sun, Tita May's sharp sympathy.

"Heidi, she seemed okay," I said. "I know you're worried, but it honestly sounds like she could be grieving. Maybe it took more time for her to process. It's not linear."

I sidestepped Tito's name. I didn't want to hear it. It sounded like a ball skittering along the floor, its rebounds making dull echoes until it would be perfectly still.

"It's more like a spiral," I said. "But it will be the up-going kind. Like a staircase. Don't worry."

"I don't know," Heidi said. Her eyes disconnected. "She's not herself."

I wanted to bring Heidi closer to me, kiss her head and

smooth her hair, but she wouldn't look at me.

Scott and Dan had graduated to a hug when we said good-bye. My mother kissed me again and said, "I'm very proud of you, *anak*. You are really trying and working hard. Congratulations on the fellowship."

Her words felt like blessing in this mood. Ally and Scott got into the car first. Before the door closed, they started whispering in their visibly confidential way.

Tita May pulled me aside, her eyes flirtatious as usual. Dan had done well. "You see him sometimes?"

Dan was standing a few feet away. Maybe Heidi was right about Tita May.

"No, not Dan," Tita May said. She ticked her tongue impatiently. "Your *tito*. Do you ever see him?"

I drew back my hand from the fire. "No, Tita."

"No one else understands," Tita May said. "I will never see him again. I missed him at the hospital. When I got there, he was not himself anymore. Do you understand? The pictures aren't real, the video isn't real. You are the only one who can see him now."

She cradled my shoulders with her whole arm. I felt her nerves. I couldn't tell her that I had given up this past, that Tito and my father weren't in them anymore, less than they were in pictures. Seeing them alive and unknowing was worse, their faces untroubled or troubled with ordinary things that all passed and died with them.

Dan hugged Heidi. "Bye, Erning," he said. "Nice to meet you finally."

"What else did you and Mom talk about?" Heidi said. "I guess you're one of us now that you know my secret name. Nobody calls me that anymore."

When Heidi was born, Tita May decided that she resembled an uncle whose own public name was Ernesto and private name was Junjun. Newborns resemble most old men, and Heidi had outgrown the resemblance. Any family tree of ours would be a tangle of private and public names. The names, and what and where we wanted to be called, walled neat compartments between time and countries. My mother's nickname, Ally, was an exception.

"Why is it a secret?" Tita May asked. "You are Erning to me still."

"Not a secret," Heidi said. "Ernesto was Mom's favorite uncle."

"He was a journalist in the revolution, a hero," Tita May said. Heidi nodded, and I felt the old pride. We were used to hearing about our unseen family as mythology. Scott rapped on the inside of the car window. My mother hit ignition.

"To be continued," Tita May said. She swung into the car. "Cliffhanger! That is your incentive if you continue to date Martha." She laughed in her usual clucking way. "Martha, no spoilers!"

Like other immigrants and families we knew, we had grown up with heroes, shadow people who had given their voices first to the fights of their times and then to our parents. Underneath their names, we had stories that we polished like silver until the smallest piece or word was enough to live on. Our own children would polish down these treasures until they were smaller and more precious. Heidi and I used to wonder if we were like them, and sometimes I thought we were.

# Chapter 12

Lolo Junjun sang "Tie A Yellow Ribbon Round the Ole Oak Tree" at rallies. It was our first story of him. Our mothers told us that he was chosen for his voice, and Heidi and I thought that the voice on the radio was his. We wore out his cassette tape. He pleaded with the bus driver and held his breath. My mother told us the lyrics until they became a myth in themselves. A man rides the bus after doing his time in prison. He will come home if his love still wants him, if she ties a yellow ribbon on the tree. When I was young, I got stuck on the lady. She tied a hundred ribbons when one would have brought him home. I understood better after my father left. I would have done anything if I knew he was even looking at a tree.

The bouncy rhythm gave away the ending. Lolo's voice, perfect on the cassette, was desperate to me, like he really had nowhere else to go. That pained voice over the sunny beat mixed me up. Heidi and I didn't dance to the song, which was odd because we danced to everything then. But we took turns singing to each other, trying to convince the love to want us. In the song, the rest of the bus riders cheer when they see, and I imagined what they would have done if the tree had been bare. When we were a bit older, we learned that all the ribbons hadn't made a difference. The man got out of the plane and was shot in the head. I got stuck on the lady again and saw her waiting.

The night I met Lolo Junjun, hot rain came down in sheets. I still remember the green gate screaming over the storms. He undid its many locks. Inside, he called me Alma, which rankled and flattered me. He wasn't calling me pretty, but he said my mother had been ugly at my age, which cheered me up. I had decided to visit Lolo for my eleventh birthday, when any mother or father seems like an ancient, and I already saw that Lolo was young. His hair was jet black, the dimensional kind that can't come out of a box, and he stood trim in a lounging sweater. He brought me chocolate milk and pulled out a spiral-bound notebook from his back pocket. He had to get the scoop. The hand that held his pen trembled, leaving scribbles on the page as he interviewed me. I reminded him I was only eleven before I answered him who would die and live. He didn't ask about himself, and I hated to force the point, but it was my reason for coming after all.

"I came to warn you, Lolo," I said. "Nobody was able to find you. They think you were killed. If you keep writing, you're going to disappear like the rest."

"Oh, my darling," Lolo said. "I know all that already."

# WINTER QUARTER: CLOSED EYES AND CANDY

# Chapter 13

My mother knocked on my door, and I assured her that I was a student post-finals, not depressed. The end of fall quarter had been one thing after another, and I couldn't remember the last time I got a good night's sleep. I slept off the studying for five days, accepting only food. When I woke up, it was to weeks of peace and boredom, since Scott and I had broken our grudge. It was strange to see him walking around the house freely. He waved when we crossed paths. I reached into myself for indignation and came up empty-handed.

Like last winter break, I didn't have any friends, but this winter I didn't have voices and madness. Alone with a still mind, I found out I needed a hobby. I fixed myself snacks while I tried knitting, karate, and indoor gardening. I gave up the rest and fixed snacks with all my time. Cooking gave me something to text Tina. Her replies dragged my heartstrings and fingers; my hands left the stovetop to text back promptly. Sometimes I burned food in efforts to keep our conversation going. I boiled spaghetti and blended lentils with ginger and cumin for a sauce. Scott ate appreciatively while my mother made rice for the real dinner. My mother took me to church with her, and I tried to look clean, contented, and busy. Her friends pinched my face and told me how worried they no

## Chapter 13

longer were.

Even on days when I didn't cook, Tina checked in with me. The questions were the same as in our room, but asking felt important since we chose it this time. I tried to check in with her, but she talked about her parents like she had already confided their history to me. I reread old texts to see if I missed something. It was possible I forgot, but Tina never said in her texts why she hated them. On top of everything, Victor was spending too much time with their parents again, according to Tina. She didn't understand how he could. Navigating this swampiness was complicated. I got by with emojis, usually food-related, which always pleased Tina. If I asked any sensible question, her replies died. But for the first time, it seemed she'd tell me someday if I kept it up.

My mother and Scott liked Dan, so I didn't get a break. I was barely used to hearing our future from Dan's lips, so their fantasies smothered me. Our relationship felt as intense as the recoil from school. I didn't have much to tell Dan when we weren't in the middle of shared experience, but I wasn't worried. I had seen we'd share years, so I knew we couldn't run out of conversation. Over the phone, I realized how much he relied on monosyllabic answers, especially since his face couldn't speak for him. When my mother asked what Dan was up to, I had monosyllabic answers.

I wasn't sure if I was going to ruin Christmas. It was too early to bet on a good mood for the exact day. We all saw the day coming steadily and implacably. The tree, wreaths, and *parol* went up. My mother brought the *parol* from the Philippines before I was born. In some places, the raw light bulbs shined through cracks in the seashell. The anticipation weighed on me, especially the lights of the *parol* that either flashed manically or shut off. Nothing in between. Sometimes I thought the memory of last year had already ruined

Christmas. The day came to us, and we didn't move a bit. We didn't breathe all Christmas, but it came and went happily because we had pulled it off that year.

With my grades being shit, I really needed to do well with this fellowship if I wanted to make something of myself. If my professors were right, the final papers I had written in such a good mood were part nonsense. Still, I wasn't worried because my project had been original. If I started during winter break, I would have a leg up on everybody by weeks at least.

I cleared off childhood paraphernalia (snail paperweight, framed photo of myself at an aquarium, pile of rejected diaries) from the desk in my bedroom. For some reason, on the day I submitted the application, I also mailed a copy to my mother's address. She left it unopened on my desk with the rest of my mail. I had stuck a stamp with a seal, perched on a pedestal with a ball on its nose, onto the envelope's backside opening. It wasn't like me to waste a stamp. I ripped off the top of the envelope and started to read.

*Nature mediates man's relationship to himself. Yet the nature of this relationship, whether to denature or in departure, delimits nature in itself. Nature delineates while man makes sex, war, et cetera. In war, the lines of nature meet the lines of soldiers, the front part of which is the front line. Lines, being the first dimension, contain infinite points; the scoreboard in war is therefore infinite. In other words, victory and loss are fundamentally uncountable but not unfeelable. Nature restores feeling to man. In consideration, my project unites the common infinity in nature and war.*

*I think everybody agrees that if the trees had been mobilized, they would have joined the Allies in World War Two. Just open your window! Ultimately, the Maginot Line failed because it left the Ardennes Forest unfortified. We let the true*

## Chapter 13

*sleeping giant hit the snooze button. Big mistake. Frequently, the first step to correcting mistakes is erasure. The original aspect of this project is that it never erases. Rather, it will fortify.*

*I will replace the phloem, xylem, syrup, et cetera within a single tree with metal. Every tree has holes inside which can be widened and filled with metal. The first step of my independent research, if funded by this fellowship, will determine the optimal combination of tree and metal. I'm thinking 100 percent gold and coastal redwood. But I am open-minded. The artistic fusion of tree and metal, a new alloy, is a monument to war produced by man and nature alike and the potential of this partnership, specifically in World War Two.*

My body got very hot when I ripped up the paper. I ripped up the cross-section of a redwood tree's rings, with years of war highlighted in gold. I had made a veined leaf out of tinfoil, and I tore the foil into sharp bits. I pulled out a diagram for an interactive display: children tapped syrup out of metal trees. They wore welding gloves to pour the molten metal on pancakes. I cut up the diagram with scissors. I kept the pop-up book of the Giant's Tomb in the Ardennes, a real place where river circles a forested hill. I peeled gold stickers off the photo.

The childhood trash around me was clearer than my fellowship proposal. I remembered that the proposal was always supposed to be lighthearted. The night I wrote it up, I couldn't stop laughing. But I had seen myself thinking on a razor's edge, landing on the side of safety and brilliance, and now the envelope opened in a spray of blood.

"I am doomed," I cried over the phone. Dan listened to me snuffle. "Who the hell would fund this project? Are they crazy or something?"

"I thought you knew it was funny," Dan said. "The

whole time I thought it was the satirical kind of joke. Tongue-in-cheek. Like a lampoon on the insanity of war, the arbitrariness. Kurt Vonnegut stuff." I couldn't follow what he was saying.

"I don't know," I said. "I don't think I was in my right mind at the time."

"It's really imaginative," Dan said. "All of it is interesting, even the parts that don't make sense. I think the fellowship people saw how creative you are."

"Whatever I was going for, I don't see it," I said. "How am I going to work on a project when I don't know what I was thinking?" Dan didn't say anything. I would scream.

"It's embarrassing," I said. "I thought I came up with something great, and it's all ridiculous. I was proud of it."

"Maybe you need to think about it concretely," Dan said. "If you break it down into a plan, you'll feel more confident. The proposal is just a concept. You'll make something real out of it."

Scott came into the room with concern, seeing me sitting among garbage. I hung up the phone and went to dinner. My mother served meatloaf with quail eggs, my favorite. The eggs popped in my mouth.

"It's art, *anak*," my mother said. "What do you expect? You are making it for yourself." She spoke soothingly, as if my ego was something holy.

I sat with a notebook. In the hospital, the art therapist printed sheets of mandala patterns for coloring. The patterns looked like mazes. Some of us were allowed to bring the sheets and crayons into therapy groups. I traced the petals and circles while the group leader taught the patients how to get better. Other people were told off for doodling, but I was an exception. Showing up was the most I could do for anybody else.

# Chapter 14

When I told classmates I took a gap year, people wished they got a chance to be free. "What did you do with your gap year?" they asked. I told them I was sick. I didn't learn new things or help people. For a while, I did email the local convent to investigate the option of becoming a silent nun. I was having trouble talking coherently at the time, and it seemed like a kind of life I could manage. I read about their strict-sounding entry processes, which involved a lot of talking, and felt disappointed again. I avoided the head nun's calls.

I learned how to salvage my answer about the gap year. "I was mostly sick. I did take an art class once." Their envy reassured, my classmates asked about my medium and subjects. I painted flowers. Scott dropped me off at the studio every week, and he waited in the parking lot until class was over. He parked as close as possible to the door and moved the car when a closer spot opened up. He watched for me in the line of exiting artists, and I didn't get any moment to run away. It was easy to tolerate him because the new medication had me stoned. I moved too slowly to run away.

My mother hung one of the flower paintings in the living room. It existed in some strange pocket in time, where I forgot I made it until I saw it. The flower I chose was green all over, a trailing vine with a puppet mouth. It was a jolly art class because everyone knew each other, except for me and another woman. She said nothing and painted a perfect bird of paradise from memory.

When I returned to school, I brought one of my paintings. It wasn't a flower, so I didn't know when I made it. Maybe we had extra time in art class one day, or maybe I sleep-painted. It was flames or mountains. The paint shattered out from the center, like a strong person slammed a fist, and the sprays of paint stopped dead midair. In between, the canvas was white as a star. I knew the painting came after the class at least because the art teacher taught us that blank canvas wasn't allowed. It had to be white. I thought I remembered filling in the cracks with the smallest brush. Tina touched the ridges made from paint slapped with a knife.

"How did you think of this?" Tina said. "I don't even know what it looks like. I love it."

"It's the only good thing I did last year," I said. "Happy birthday." Her birthday was in a few weeks, but it would be hard to hide a painting from my roommate.

"I can't take your painting," Tina said. "It means a lot to you." She distracted me with chocolate bars and a wrapped gift. I didn't open them.

"I really want you to have the painting."

She held the canvas by its edges. She stared hard, like she was trying to place it. "It's beautiful, Martha. Thank you." She propped it on her desk against the frame of her bunk bed. She set her brain candle in front of the painting. The smashed flames lit the candle.

"The gift is from my parents," Tina said. "They said to tell you it's a Christmas present." Wrapping paper puckered at the corners of the box.

It was a tiny bearded bean.

## Chapter 14

"It's a metal seed," Tina said. "They really liked the idea for your project."

"Seriously?" The silver seed sat in the box. It looked like a bug egg. "Well, thank them for me," I said. She didn't talk to her parents. I should have asked Victor to thank them.

"You could put it on a chain and wear it as a necklace," Tina said.

I pulled out a bracelet with charms. The seed didn't have any loops or hooks, and it was too slippery for duct tape. I stuck it in the bottom of my front pants pocket. It gave a shock of cold when I touched it. I held it in a fist at fellowship orientation that afternoon, switching hands when I introduced myself.

I already forgot the room while I was in it. It looked like every place on campus, either over-bright with windows or carpeted in some kind of absorbent wool. I expected to see tall people, vests, and plastic cups. The door was already open, so I didn't get a chance to gather myself. Entering doorways into a crowd had to be my worst activity. More than anything, I hated the view of people's hair becoming face when they turned to me as a collective. Most, I hated how their eyes, in turning, stayed insensate as they met mine, flicking away almost immediately. The greatest relief came when nobody's head rotated at all. I slipped into my seat.

The circle of students sat forward in our plastic stackable chairs, so our heads made a tight inner circle like a knot of synchronized swimmers. I recognized a boy from my Philosophy classes, who wore combat boots and shell earrings. In every class, he asked whether we were actually talking to each other, or if we were brains floating around in jars. He voted for jars.

"Welcome, fellows. My name is Emma Todd-Hannibal," said the oldest woman.

It was impossible to tell her age. Her hair, dyed maroon, could have been white or green underneath. She dressed as a flower child recast for a corporate librarian, with a sweater cut as a suit and a poppy in her hair. She didn't stand and talked to us from among our circle, now and then fixing on a single person for paragraphs. Her blue eyes, overdrawn with eyeliner that left a moon of white skin in between, were framed in glasses that she'd switch out constantly, each pair more presciently stylish than the last.

"All of you were selected for disruptive promise. We look for students who will undermine civilization. People with the powers to ruin everything, but who choose to create something. In our judgment, we evaluated your applications. Unbeknownst to any of you, we also considered input from secret informers throughout campus."

The girl across from me became pink and soft. I imagined Dr. Walsh informing Emma Todd-Hannibal.

"Each of you shows potential to challenge thought leaders in your destined fields. In addition to your qualities for innovation, we asked ourselves, 'Who really wants this opportunity? Who needs this chance to make something of themselves?' We believe desperation becomes drive. Mass desperation becomes society. Let's introduce ourselves now, please."

I don't know why we had to sit in circles at the hospital. I used to think the shape tried to make us all equal, but the hospital was no place for empowerment. Somebody is always staring at somebody in a circle. Maybe it was for accountability. In the hospital, a person can go anywhere, as long as they don't mind being trapped. I couldn't get up from this circle without attracting Emma's eyes. I wished we all wore patients' scrubs, which made us gentler with each other. It was hard to be too judgmental when we sat around in body bibs, a snap clasp away from bare-bottoming the chairs. I looked around this circle, our first session.

New intakes have an earnest look or else stare past walls. Sometimes they inject speedy friendliness into the group, which we all know will soon be medicated. Some of us sit in drugged speechlessness. People about to leave have loafing eyes because they don't care about us anymore. People who stay long enough might make friends, pinch off into a cranny, and have laughs too loud to be sane. If anybody wants to get discharged, they have to earn points in the group leader's clipboard. It's easy to get points because wanting points means a kind of rationality already. Group leaders like rationality, except for Emma. We were all new intakes here, and I wondered how the ideas that flew in frantic energies could land.

"I'm Hank. My project is to create flags for all 196 countries using a universal palette. I'm feeling energized by all of you today, so I'm a 9 out of 10."

"Hi, Rosie here. I'm really interested in community, so I'm conducting an ethnography of dog shows. Unfortunately, I have a stomach virus, so I put myself at a 2 out of 10."

"I'm Hector, going to build a museum of synesthesia. I disagree with rating myself."

"Hey, everyone, my name's Anita. I'm going to a raise a turtle for forty years. I'm an 8."

"Hi, all. Liz. If the Epic of Gilgamesh can be written on stone tablets, why not bell hooks? I'm feeling a 6 right now."

"My name is Leila. My project is to conduct an orchestra of broken instruments. It'll take a bit of tuning, that's for sure. I rate myself 10 out of 10 for the moment."

"Dev. Really fascinated by Russian mud. I think I'm about a 5, right in the middle."

"Hello, my name is Estelle. I'm going to bartend in Antarctica, so you won't see much of me this year. I'm worried about my project, so I'm a 5 out of 10."

"Hey, I'm Carson. Looks I'm the only techie in the group. I'm interested in machine learning to write fellowship applications. I don't understand this scale."

"Thomas. Faces. 8.5."

The circle closed, and the faces swung to me, the new pinwheel. I waited for the group leader to bring some of these fancies back to the point, but Emma puffed up with each new monologue. Nobody got in trouble. If the group leader smiled enough, offenders settled back into harmlessness or hopelessness, both silent. Other times leaders mowed down digressions. I started a nice discussion once about whether the voices talked in code or if their language was the mother language, but it was shut down before we broke through.

"Hi, I'm Martha. I would say I'm feeling about a 7 out of 10. I was going to make an art piece of metal trees and war, but I was actually wondering if it's possible for me to refocus my topic." It was the wrong kind of disruption.

"Absolutely," Emma said. She smiled at me with doughy pleasantness. "We're investing in you, not your ideas. What is your idea?"

"I was thinking of doing an oral history of Filipino immigrants to the United States," I said.

Emma squeezed her eyes and pulled petals from the poppy in her hair. "What does everyone think?" she said. "I'm part of the status quo, so let's hear from you all."

"It's not very specific at this point," I said. "I can time travel, and I'm really interested in families through generations. I think there's a link there. I'm not sure what to expect from the interviews, so I thought I could pick out themes once I hear from people about their experiences." I was a

## Chapter 14

word away from convincing everyone, but it wasn't a word I knew.

"My project has a similar inductive approach," Estelle said. Her voice lilted; everybody's did. "I don't know what to expect in Antarctica, either."

"I like it. I think it's very meaningful," said Hank. "I just don't know if it's going to upend technology." He shook his head sympathetically.

"We're supposed to be kind of disrupting systems," Carson agreed.

"What was your other idea?" Thomas asked. He held a mask of my face, pasted on a popsicle stick, in front of his. His eyes looked out from my nostril slits.

"Metal trees in the Ardennes Forest," I said. "The idea of fortifications, nature, war." I squeezed the silver seed, but it was too small and hard to absorb my stress.

"Well, that's a lot more specific," Rosie said. She showed me a picture of a fluff-chinned dog.

"And fascinating," said Hank. He pulled out the old and new flags of Canada from his backpack.

"Perhaps there is a way," Emma said, "you can transfuse the new idea into the old. Oral history trees. Culture wars. Immigration of metals."

Emma wrote the words on a whiteboard and connected them with squiggles. She drew a spasm of fire around. Now and then, an outstanding group leader became the fixation of our affections, usually for treating us as human beings. Emma didn't seem to think we were human. She acted like our skin glowed.

"Thanks for your help," I said. "I'll definitely work on it."

All the words from everybody went down easy. Our chairs scooted closer to each other and the circle's hub. We passed around props from our projects, and Hank brought out a brain in a jar.

"In any case, Martha, we would appreciate it if your new product privileged your original idea," Emma said. "We are required to have a proportion of physical arts pieces every year among our recipients, and we were counting on at least a metal tree. The exact symbolism is up to the artist."

"I see," I said. "Okay, tree it is."

I thought about planting the metal seed under dirt for my art piece. I had looked carefully at trees and metal lately, and I didn't see how the smooth planes could become something living.

"Today was a superb start," Emma said. "I am so empowered to see you talking to each other. I remain your ready assistant for all things related to your fellowship and creation generally. I hope you come to see this group as a core of the revolution." She passed around business cards embossed with mangoes.

Hank fingered his shell earring and drummed his knuckles against his boot. "What I've been wondering this whole time," he started, "is whether we are even talking to each other at all. Or if we're all just brains floating in jars sending and receiving impulses." It was Estelle's turn to hold the brain in a jar. She shook it hard, like she was practicing to make cocktails in Antarctica.

Emma sat up. "Now, that's disruptive." She smoothed her socks and stared at Hank with deep interest. I remembered a friend in the hospital, who, on his first day, convinced us that we were all part of his virtual reality machine. The staff dissuaded us before they realized that we were deeply comforted.

"The way I see it," Hank said, "I don't think a brain in a body should have more rights than a brain in a jar." He

## Chapter 14

looked to me for support. I had heard his line of thinking many times in class, and the repeated sounds had become nonsensical. Thomas switched to a mask of Hank's face.

I had stayed long enough to make a friend, and I pinched off with Estelle to walk home. She worried about which of the two bars in Antarctica would give a better experience for her project. Gallagher's Pub was a family-owned operation, and she always wanted to support local businesses. I had absolutely no opinion, but I tried to sympathize. It felt like my first day the first time I lived in the locked unit, when the surreal movie scenes dissolved into daily practicalities: shower slippers, the good kind of toothbrush, whether I swallowed pills one at a time or threw them back all at once. It was the same kind of drama I found myself in now, what happened before good people got better. How they pissed away their time, practicing passion for whatever they would eventually find worth dying for. All of them grew up and found it, but not yet.

# Chapter 15

As soon as Tina told me she quit choir, I remembered I forgot to. "I emailed Marsha and told her I don't have time," she said. "Medical schools don't give you a pass after first quarter." Cream cheese slipped off of her bagel and into the book she studied. She shrugged.

My mind always finds space for a worry, a pocket for panic that doubles into itself until the whole brain can live in this dirty vesicle. I congratulate myself for staying away from a thought, and I return to a bigger dread. Marsha could throw me out, and I'd keep walking. Until then, her face followed me whether I laughed or stared. Everyone in the dorm talked about our ski trip while I chanted lines of my email. People drew out the preparations to have something to say until I knew everyone's packing list. Tina overheard my muttering and shook her head.

"Marsha will be mad, but she doesn't care either way," Tina said. "People have other things to think about." I had nothing else to think about.

"Are you sure you want to quit?" Dan said. "You're really talented. You're down on singing now, but what happens when you feel better?" He rubbed my shoulder. He didn't get that I had to minimize exposure, close all the doors to

## Chapter 15

instability.

"I'll find another way," I said. "I don't have time anymore with the fellowship. I need to make the best tree that I can. It's important to me. I need all the time."

"Music helps you cope," Dan said. "If you change your mind, you can probably come back. Maybe you can tell Marsha what's going on." I nodded.

"Marsha doesn't give a rat's ass about you," Tina said.

Dan and I packed our bags for our ski trip. The fabrics, some shiny and some pebbled, made me forget Marsha while I touched them. Dan showed me his bag, which I approved. Mutual approval danced in the air. He kissed me goodnight, and I forgot again. Tina sighed after the door closed. The room felt sealed and silent.

"Man, that guy is the worst," Tina said. She continued her complex system of highlighting. The caps clicked on and off.

"Dan?" I didn't follow. The coziness that the three of us had generated for months still clouded the room.

"Your boyfriend. He doesn't know what he's talking about. You can't tell everybody your business. He doesn't even know Marsha."

"I wouldn't tell her all my business. I'd only share what's relevant to choir." I jumped to my defense, not Dan's.

"He talks about coping skills. I hate all those fake words, the medical words. He doesn't know. You like music. That's all. You changed your mind. That's all." The markers squeaked on the paper.

"He didn't mean it that way. He's right. Music makes me feel better."

She kept turning up her speakers while we argued. Her voice got louder and louder to carry over the song. I wasn't sure who she was talking to anymore. The music was too loud for her to go on. She plugged in her headphones, and the brief screech as the music shifted over became silence again.

Tina's rotten mood layered bad feelings on top of mine. The choir wouldn't have enough voices, and I needed to clear up that I was the one who wanted to quit first. People would think—and I felt the crush of people's thoughts, even if they weren't formed yet—that I was a person to die if I didn't have a friend. I typed a short email to Marsha that could seem rushed, like I wasn't worried to the point of carelessness. It was better to be unclear. Ambiguity put me in the higher, more knowledgeable position. I sent the email when my schedule allowed me to wait around for a couple hours afterwards. She replied eighteen hours later: *OK. well talk after rehearsal tomorrow. find me.*

Tina wasn't helpful in interpretation. I tried to decipher whether "after rehearsal" was meant to specify the time only. Or if Marsha expected me to go to rehearsal first, which seemed patently insane. I ran through either scenario and decided I had to avoid the moment where I waited for Voices of Reason to finish. I saw myself running into everybody as we passed each other in the door. It couldn't happen. On to the next calamity. Would I tell everybody I was going to quit? My heart told me no. But I imagined, clear as day, Kara's expression of confusion when I'd see her around campus. She was unavoidable. They all were.

Or maybe not. Maybe I'd graduate without seeing any of them again. It could be possible if I didn't leave my room as much. I wouldn't say anything for now. If I saw anybody again, I'd explain that I hadn't decided yet at rehearsal and made up my mind when I met with Marsha afterwards. No point in telling people uncertainties. I might still change my mind anyway. Marsha would explain somehow without me.

## Chapter 15

Maybe it'd be better if she told everybody since she was the boss.

Marsha and I sat at a picnic table outside the building where we sang. Rehearsal wasn't so bad. I had experimented with an absorbed expression, like the craft of music was carrying me away. I mostly ignored people's talking voices. When I didn't respond, opportunities for conversation almost disappeared. The picnic table felt unprofessional. The splinters chafed my butt.

"We won't have enough people. Tina quits, then you," Marsha said. She kept talking, and I couldn't interrupt. "You could start a domino effect. I've seen it other years."

"I don't have time, Marsha. I'm sorry," I said. "The fellowship ties me up now. I wish I wasn't so busy. It was really fun sometimes." I remembered our first rehearsals. Dan had reminded me.

"It doesn't have to end. You sounded great today. I know I got mad over the incident at the fall show. I can be uptight, but I'm forgiving." She smiled with benevolence. "I have a short memory. Honestly, I've barely thought about it since."

"It doesn't have to do with you," I said. I read graffiti on the picnic table.

"If it's a scheduling issue, you could take a break and come back. I've done that arrangement before."

I needed to slam all the doors to my volatile place. "I shouldn't sing anymore," I said. I watched myself silent from a long distance. Marsha waited for an apology.

"It's your decision," she said. She sighed. I smiled with absoluteness and shifted on the splinters.

"The other reason I wanted to meet with you, Martha," Marsha began. "I've been thinking. I wanted to ask you if you're doing quite okay?"

I watched myself frozen from a long distance. "I'm fine." I knew what she saw, and I sat up straighter.

"Okay, okay." Marsha pushed her palms at me, a shrug on my behalf. "I had a difficult freshman year myself."

I thought she must be lying, but she smirked sadly.

"No, it's a scheduling issue," I said. I met her eyes fully, like a sane person would.

"Well, I'm around," Marsha said. She pushed off the table.

Dan applauded the assertiveness we had practiced. Tina said nothing. She stared at the road as she drove. Dan sat in the backseat. He leaned forward until his clapping hands were next to our faces. I missed Tina's good mood, so I chose the front seat next to her. Before we left, she told me not to think about what she said.

"I'm used to being around people I don't like," Tina said in our room. She locked the door on our way out.

Dan hugged me tightly, first wrapping his arms around the chair and then across my shoulders.

"I thought you didn't want me to quit," I said.

"I love you," Dan said. "I want you to get what you want."

"I have a lot of homework," Tina said. I followed her eyes, but the road was straight and empty.

"Good," I said. "I wanted to work on my project." Since I hadn't started the machine work yet, I could research from anywhere, as long as I had my phone or laptop. I was still in the design stage, where I looked at as many trees as possible.

"Nobody's going to ski?" Dan said. He tried for a game tone and overshot, sounding like a clown on a cliff.

"I've never been skiing before," Tina said.

Dan's breaths were audible. Usually, he breathed through his nose. "Why are we going then?"

## Chapter 15

"I've never seen snow before," Tina said.

She was smiling at the road.

Our dorm disembarked into a cluster of cabins. Icy crust made pulverizing noises as we walked on the grass. People stared for a moment, collectively approving of the snow and situation generally. The minute of appreciation became anxiety, as the crowd agitated toward friends and friends' cabins. I followed Tina, who had sprung into action. She pushed our way to a bedroom. She folded her clothes into the drawers, while Dan and I questioned each other with our eyes.

"Martha, you can stay with me if you want," Tina said.

"You should try to find a bed, Dan," I said. The crowd's agitation already slowed as the winners and losers settled in.

"I brought a sleeping bag," Dan said. "I'll crash under the pool table. Not everybody's going to get a bed."

"You're going to be so uncomfortable. Why don't you check the other cabins? They knew how many people were coming. I'm sure they got enough room for us."

"I don't think so." Dan referenced an upperclassman, which settled most of our questions, who had told him ski trip was uncomfortable and weird.

"Why are we going then?" Tina said.

"To ski." Dan snapped on his ski goggles and mimed swishing down slopes. His eyes behind the goggles were opaque and holographic. "Are you sure you don't want to ski?"

"We'll go outside later," I said. I sat next to Tina, who scooted over to receive me with a smile. I knew the look of her books as well as I knew mine, and she produced them suddenly as though they had been behind my ears the whole time. It was Tina's magic trick.

The other Bond-Rummy fellows had incredible taste in music, and I keyed up the best playlist I ever made. On shuffle, the effect was dizzying. The thought of the playlist helped me get up in the morning. The sound must potentiate my work, I thought, so I listened to a few tracks every day before starting my research. The list of essential preparatory tracks got longer and longer. I sat with my headphones for thirty minutes before turning off the music. I hadn't exactly achieved the right mood, but I was working on a deadline.

The challenging part of design is whether to start with the idea or with the limits of what's possible, given current understanding of physics and biology. I asked Emma.

"Do you have to pick one, Martha? Doesn't disruption demand, to some extent, misunderstanding of possibility?"

It would have been rude to repeat her questions back to her, so I nodded and tried to do both. I made a chart of all the types of trees I could find. Some types were pinned with leaves that I had collected on hikes. I used some of my grant money to travel to Indianapolis, where I visited a museum with a metal tree. From this experience, I gathered that I wanted my tree to be much taller and more realistic, which the other fellows agreed with. I watched many World War Two documentaries and took notes on any trees I saw. I used more grant money to buy a small notebook that fit into my pocket, so I could pull it out in case I got inspiration walking around. It was a little more expensive, but I got a nice notebook that flipped upwards instead of sideways, like Lolo Junjun's notebook. I took it out of my back pocket now and reviewed my notes from the last week. They were fragments, but I thought the act of observing was creative.

Tina nodded along with her own music, and the flip of the flashcards got into a speedier rhythm. She dealt the deck into four hands. She kept a poker face and sighed as the game ended.

"Dan's right," Tina said. "We need to get out of here."

## Chapter 15

She'd borrowed my warmest Midwestern coat, so I walked next to a mattress on leggings. White crunch got everything's corners furry. The air went straight to our lungs and iced every cell on its way inside. Falling snow pulled down sun. Light stacked around us. Tina smiled tightly, and I saw the tightness came from hiding a bigger smile. In between the flakes, the lights hung thin and fine. We stomped down the clouds of our second, grounded sky.

"What'd you think of snow, Tina?" Dan asked over dinner. The frozen pizzas came out of the oven. The cabin smelled like pepperoni and hormones. Someone turned off a lamp in a corner of the room, and bodies twisted to the music, staying in the limits of the darkness. Dan said the slopes had been perfect, hot enough to warm but not to melt.

"It was a pretty great day," Tina said.

"And how'd your fellowship work go, Martha?" Dan crunched on the pizza that was somehow both soggy and dry as a cracker. The other dorm-mates quieted, starting to listen in. We were always vigilant for genius among us, so we could catch some ourselves.

"Honestly, it's coming together really slowly. I'm still conceptualizing, and it's taking longer than I thought. I could take it in a lot of different directions, and I don't know where to go next."

The dorm-mates tuned in. We collected seeds of prodigy in each other. They asked me if I knew people, a metallic product designer, a kinetic artist in residence, a scholar of botanic wars, a pastor, a tree-climbing champion in Dan's dorm. It was freshman year, when we helped each other know people.

"Thanks, guys. You're right, I should talk to as many people as I can," I said. Dan nodded many times.

"It's such an interesting concept. I love the symbolism.

You're doing what I've always wanted to do," a girl said.

"I told everybody about your project. Everybody's intrigued," a guy said.

Dan craned his arm around me, and the hug was buffered with our sweaters and scarves. We didn't need them, but it was fun to feel seasonal.

"Martha is so imaginative," he said. "She gets these crazy ideas all the time. She'll make connections out of nowhere. I couldn't come up with the stuff she thinks about. She makes my life fun. I don't know who I would be without her."

He would have gone on, but I elbowed him. As a dorm, we hadn't decided the limits for our precocious couples. It wasn't nice to brag.

Too many people couldn't be kept apart, so our over-full cabin became sweaty with people and layers. A group of us took up too much space working on a jigsaw puzzle, and sleepy drunk people started to complain behind our backs. It was a devilish puzzle of infinitely stacked pencils, and the academic theme stressed us out. Some kind of confrontation broke out between the sober puzzle-doers and drunk sleepers, and I left.

Dan and Tina spoke too steadily. Their low voices stood out among the laughing and fun tones. I was hearing them before I could turn around. The room was so crowded that I couldn't get away once I figured out I wanted to. I looked at the floor to give them some privacy that their lowness assumed.

"You treat her like she's sick. She's an adult, and she's fine the way she is."

"I'm not going to sit back and watch her struggle."

"Who's sitting back? I've known her longer than you have. She's been this way the whole time."

I didn't have to push away because their voices stopped.

# Chapter 16

"It wasn't right for us to talk about you behind your back," Tina said.

She'd never been one to repeat herself, but now she asked for the same forgiveness every time we ran into each other. I slept at Dan's more and more. I gave her the forgiveness she wanted, but it was charity, too selfless to last. We didn't get what we missed: the old companionable air. Silence became silence, flat, not the rests between upbeats we used to have. I would have forgiven her if she asked right. I still saved it for her.

I came back for clothes and pills. I tucked the orange pill bottle into a bunch of underwear and talked loudly, throwing my voice to the door before I walked out. Tina wouldn't disagree with pills. She agreed with action, forcefully taken. I'd taken the pills, but the forces behind them were Dan, who pressured me into destigmatizing myself, and Dr. Walsh, who didn't know how they worked but knew how people told her they felt.

I breathed deeply walking down the hall. My dorm-mates would ask me where I'd been, and I'd run out of breath explaining, so I needed to save up. Dan and I practiced breathing in the evenings before sleeping. I put a hand on my gut, where Dr. Walsh showed me, and watched my hand rise slowly as I filled my lungs. I must have been breathing wrong because my gut didn't leave any air for my lungs. I coughed. Coughing slowed me down, and I had to get out of the dorm before anyone saw me.

Dr. Walsh and Dan said the breathing would help me stay in the present, same as the pills. I tried to read Dr. Walsh's eyes to see which I should take. She explained people told her all the ways helped at different times in their lives. I didn't have time to wait for another time in my life, so I took all the ways. Dan gave me a mood chart that I filled out after we practiced breathing. I usually felt a bit better after breathing, so I was pleased to see my high scores.

The present felt closer since the pills and charts and coughing, but it pulled me down into its plodding details, while I kicked toward the sky. Seen from below, the world reduced to blurs and colors so bright they hurt me all over. I was sinking more each day; my gravity was reversing from the sun to the ground. I wanted to sink. I wanted to be at the same level as everyone I loved. But the absence of the more extraordinary life cut into me. If I could still time travel, I would skip the withdrawal pains, to the new and lower stability everyone wanted.

One or all of the ways was working, because I made many decisions without regret. Or joy, either. I guessed this is what a level head felt like. I chose Dan without panic. He wanted to help me, and Tina didn't. A simple analysis of what I overheard showed me the split that separated them. And I needed help.

When Heidi invited me to her science fair, I agreed, even though three weeks was too much time to guess what my mood would be. Depending on the day, a week's notice could be pushing it. But the pills got me feeling reliable every time

## Chapter 16

I remembered to take them.

"I know you're really busy. Isn't it exams? You don't have to come. My research is pretty technical. They don't give us enough time for background. Only twelve minutes. It's not a presentation for laypeople. And then they make it open to the public. It's stupid actually. You won't understand what's going on. How boring is that going to be for you? Mom said she's going to cook dinner. You could meet us at our house after the fair. Aren't you busy?"

I had been breathing deeply. I opened my eyes to the present when I heard Heidi stop talking.

"I want to support you, Heidi," I said. My level head nodded.

Dan wanted to borrow Tina's car, and I had to explain we'd get around more slowly from now on. He didn't see what the problem was if she wouldn't mind. She would mind, I told him, because I couldn't look at her. I looked at her hair instead. My eyes followed the rim of her forehead in a rolling motion. Tita May couldn't give us a ride because she was working late and didn't have time to make a stop. The trip would have two legs, three if I counted biking down Palm Drive, four if I counted walking to her school from the bus stop. We padded our schedule with twelve minutes in case the bus transfer was sloppy or our bikes jammed; we left two hours before the fair.

We walked in four minutes late. We'd taken wrong turns inside the school's halls. If the scattered audience was counted together, Heidi's talk filled at least three rows. People in California believe in buffer seats, so the ends of nine rows were taken, leaving long gaps to invade. We didn't see Tita May's hair, and I quickly calculated the backsides of heads. We scooted in front of a Filipino girl in the third row.

Heidi's suit stuck stiffly to her collar and legs. The ponytail made her moles pop out. Tita May had picked her makeup, so her lips shined with a gloss made of light pink poison. The color was right on her usual complexion, but her skin had gone pale. On the wall, the laser pointer's red dot struggled erratically.

Whatever hope I had of understanding Heidi's talk was gone with the first four minutes, five if you counted finding our seats. Every word sounded like a breakthrough. Or a robot's surname. She'd worked with a professor on the physics of time travel. Field equations, energy conservation. I was completely lost.

"I don't entirely understand the renormalization scale, but I estimate that it's not relevant for this problem," Heidi said. The judge narrowed his eyes.

I shook Dan's shoulder urgently. Some of those words were bullshit, and the judge had caught her. I clenched the metal seed, but it slipped around in my hand like a wet tear.

"Thank you all for coming to my presentation," said Heidi. She clicked to the last slide. "I especially want to thank my mother."

All the heads turned toward and past us. I looked behind. Tita May leaned against the back wall. Her shoulders bent forward until her body crumpled between their points. The dress swallowed her bones. She didn't register all the faces her way; her eyes scanned the last slide again and again. She must have put it together, because her eyes flicked to Heidi, and she smiled. Seeing Dan and me, she straightened up and waved her fingers.

"Hello, my dears," Tita May said. Heidi bent over the school's laptop, deleting and moving around files. She switched off the projector. The lights were on the other side of the room, so the room was still dim.

"I'm so sorry I couldn't pick you up. I went straight

## Chapter 16

from work, and I almost missed Erning's talk myself, as you could see for yourselves," Tita May said. She hugged me. Her embrace was always a crush of gauzy fabrics and scent of some spicy fur. I could feel her angles through her dress, and her body smelled of nothing.

"Don't worry about it. We don't mind at all. It's not a problem," Dan said.

"Erning, you have worked so hard, *anak*. I'm proud of you. Really. I don't understand a word, but it's very impressive, *anak*," Tita May said. She pinched Heidi's forearm. "This girl has written a sixty-page paper. Sixty-one? Your Tito Rickyboy is asking for a copy, by the way. He is a professor in chemical physics. Tenured."

Heidi had walked out before she finished talking. Tita May lingered in the room before trailing Dan and me as if on a long, lazy leash.

"You remember Tito Rickyboy, girls. He used to babysit you when you were young. He was always very bright. But, Erning, you are even brighter than him. I can't wait to see where you will go in life. And I'm coming with you. You won't forget about me when you're famous, will you? I know you won't."

Her voice floated on the linoleum while her steps clicked faster after us.

"Before I forget. Martha, talk to my friend about your project. He's a veteran, so he knows. Arthur will help you. Don't forget about him. He's going to love you. He's waiting for you. Hurry up, okay? I know you're having fun, but you need to get serious. You see, I can help you still. My god, you're an artist in the family. I've always wanted an artist in the family. Imagine!" Candy wrappers and receipts crackled in her bag as she fished around for a phone number to push into my hands.

"Thank you for coming, Ma," Heidi said.

"Of course I would be here. Now, the poster session is next." She stopped short of the auditorium doors, where the noise of scientists spilled out like a rock show. She rubbed her temples. "I need to go home to prepare dinner. I'm sure I can come back for the awards."

"If you're tired, you can take a rest," I said.

Tita May dropped her hands to her sides. "Why would I be tired? No, you're right, I had a long day. Maybe I will take a rest after cooking. I'll be back for the awards. I'll be right back." She touched Heidi's hand before turning down the hall.

Dan and I helped carry Heidi's poster past the rows of scientists, standing behind roped-off stanchions that separated them from the laypeople. Each board was labeled with a number, and each scientist was labeled with the same number. It could have been an orderly scene except for the sexual tension. A boy tapped Heidi on the back, and she shook him off. Unfolded, her poster board was triptych art, with swirls of derivatives for icons. We hugged her good luck and, lost in the gray matter that surrounded us, looked back. Heidi had taken a scholarly interest in another scientist's project, and we watched her drift away from her post to investigate.

We followed the crowds to the robot. Rumors flew in the air about its capabilities. It was more of a disembodied claw than a real bunch-of-bolts bot, but the mob acted like it was a celebrity. It did move and everything. It beeped as it cleaned an empty can of beans and then crushed it. It flicked the crumb of a can into the clawing audience. The scientist had been inspired by trash.

"I don't know, I think Heidi's project has more human impact," Dan said.

I didn't see any project as good as Heidi's. She had done

## Chapter 16

the most math by far. We listened to suited girls and boys describe protocols, pointing to line graphs that only went up and up. They invited us to look more closely at dotted slides of cells, which convinced me that I must be colorblind. We tripped over the stanchions sometimes, and the proctors reminded us not to touch the science.

The judges agreed. Heidi glared at a line of ogling boys as she marched to take first prize. She'd shake them off wearily until she landed a genius grant and tenure at Stanford, who threw in a house near Tita May and hired her husband, all to secure that priceless mind. On the stage, she raised her trophy. Her slight frame pretended to stumble under its weight, and she laughed with her friends. She'd tell me the moment was her flashpoint, when she saw the equations stretch into her future, unspooling into joy without answer.

"Thanks so much for coming. It means a lot to me, Martha," Heidi said. She sweated from the stage lights and tied her blazer around her waist. Dan and I helped carry Heidi's medals. "Doesn't it take you two hours to get back? You don't need to come over. It's getting late. Don't you have exams?"

"Of course we're coming," I said. "I want to say bye to your mom." I knew without checking that Tita May hadn't made it.

I wished I'd taken the wheel because the car danced as Heidi counted her victories. The judges, with their ploys, couldn't trap her. She told us answers to trick questions, how she had cleared her throat to steady her voice as she destroyed them. She was drunk. She parked in front of Tito's desk. The garage, clean as they liked everything, smelled like rotting paper. The drunk drained from Heidi's face when we saw a lump reclining in the backseat of Tita May's car. The door was locked, and Heidi rapped on the window. The lump turned. Tita May's eyes were already open.

"Jesus! I overslept. I don't know what happened." Her voice was muffled until she rolled down the window. The expression of fright didn't leave her eyes.

"Heidi won the whole thing," Dan said. He held up a handful of medals on ribbons.

"Jesus! I missed it. I can't believe it. Honestly." She smacked herself on the forehead and opened the car door.

"I don't care, Ma," Heidi said. She took Tita May's arm and led her into the house, where there were too many shadows, straight-edged and others like cloth. Whatever had been in closets and drawers cluttered the floor, left in weaving lines that lapped the furniture. I didn't know they had so much junk hidden away.

"Don't mind the *kalat*. Don't tell your mom, okay? We've been so busy," Tita May said. She pulled her arm away from Heidi's and led us into the kitchen.

"How about I order pizzas? Deep dish. You must be tired of my cooking by now. I made a cake earlier. You see, I knew you would win. And if you didn't, you would have the cake. We'll eat cake first. Come, come. We'll go upstairs." She reached into the fridge and blocked our eyes from the cake with her back.

"Mom, we don't need to go upstairs," Heidi said. "Look, I'll clear off the table." Dan and I helped her stack the newspapers, unplugged iron, and piles of slippers.

Tita May was gone. We followed her noise upstairs into Tito's office, which was its same polished self, except for the statue. The smell of incense was stronger, from the candles. She was sitting on the bed with the cake. The frosting was mocha buttercream, delicately raked on its sides into stripes. The top and bottom piping were perfectly even the whole way around, in sherbet orange and green. She had written,

## Chapter 16

"Congratulations, Erning" in flowers. She'd use the design for Heidi's wedding cake when we were a little older.

"It's really beautiful, Ma. Thank you."

"Erning, it is always my pleasure. I am so proud of you. Winning everything. I saw all the other students. You even beat Bernice Rivera? Didn't you say she goes to Harker? Imagine! How much is their tuition, Erning? And you beat them all. I'm your mother, I am allowed to brag."

The sculpture of Tito's body dripped behind her. She had changed her mind about his ears, and the layers of clay folded on top of each other, into the encrustations of his cartilage. She hadn't gotten to his eyes.

"Now, you're going to blow candles. Don't say you're too old. I'm your mother, and I made you a cake. I'm going to miss all your birthdays from now on. You'll blow on cakes when we're together."

Tita May pulled out a fat candle patterned with the Virgin Mary. Heidi blew it out gently. The room was bright anyway.

"Daddy is so proud of you."

The cake tasted as tender as any she'd made, on our birthdays and every Christmas. She swayed in her seat at the flavor. She took our plates and headed down the stairs, leaving the dishes on a side table. Heidi gave us our coats. Tita May had tied a sweater around her shoulders and smoothed my hair, smelling me.

"Let's get sushi! Whatever you want. I'll go out today. Let me put my makeup on first. I didn't have time earlier. Let me go upstairs. My god, what is this dress. I'd like to change clothes. Do you think I have time? Maybe shower. So I'll be fresh. I'll be right back. I'll meet you there. Don't wait for me." We heard the door to Tito's office open.

# Chapter 17

Tita May traveled in time. She didn't care if I told my mother or Heidi, but I wasn't allowed to tell them about her moods and ideas. I answered in whispers over the phone because she kept talking under her breath. She explained to me carefully that people had a stigma against emotion.

Tito had taken her out dancing again last night, which got her emotional. Recently, since Heidi was born, they only danced at weddings despite Tita May's desperation for more. She suspected he chose weddings to show off, and she complained that the old fun wasn't enough for him anymore. She was rustier than Tito, but she had always been worse, she admitted. They danced to their theme song for now in order to practice. She sang the words to keep the beat, which had always irritated Tito, Heidi, and me. She knew we'd do karaoke later, but she could never wait. Tita May was pleased that speaking Tagalog to a disco cadence somehow improved my accent. I searched "at isasayaw ko" for a translation, so I could match her singing spirit. I would have asked her, but she'd be sad I didn't understand. Tita May practiced on her own as well, sometimes while we were on the phone, and I could hear from her unsteady breathing that she was spinning, swinging her arms, and twitching her straight hips.

## Chapter 17

"You're lucky you got your mom's butt," she said.

Tita May had always told me euphemistically that imagination and emotion ran in our family, which my mother disagreed with, on the grounds that she didn't have any. Time travel is a lonely ability, and, as a child, I hoped it ran in our family as well. I could have made more of an effort to dig up our family history, but my mother knew mostly stories of food, Catholicism, and professional achievement. I couldn't ask my dad. Being a scaredy cat, I didn't make much of an impression with time traveling myself, so it was possible that the ability would be untraceable. I didn't see that the scaredy cat gene ran in our family, but it might associate with time travel, from my experience.

Of course, I observed that Tita May's time traveling was different from mine, had a maddeningly unspecific flavor to it. But we understand so little about the human brain. Unless she had been keeping things from us these years, the ability had arisen suddenly in her, which I didn't know was possible. I wished I could ask Heidi, who knew all about the chemical reactions I thought were at play, if anything. But I could see Tita May's judgment was impaired lately, and the time travel should stay a secret for now, even if she didn't see it that way. I hated to be paternalistic, but I had seen for myself the risk that came with disclosing, and I didn't think she could handle the stress.

Unlike my mother, Tita May kept my secrets, especially my moods and disabilities. She muttered when she talked to me, which created a cozy feeling that I had overtaken Heidi in her confidences. More than this flattery, hearing about Tito thrilled and settled me. It was a kind of intoxication. My heart would still be racing hours later, my grin persistent and silly, my mind slurring with abundance. I couldn't stand the dead stories about him, which was all we had before Tita

May's travels. My mother loves to reminisce, even about yesterday, turning over memories until they've become entirely different characters: details suddenly delightful, portentous of legend, durable with nobility. She talks as if we knew the whole time that he was going to die, like we were watching for symbolism. She doesn't see anymore that he lived in ordinary annoyances and gentle love.

Tita May's travels brought Tito back from the dead stories. He crunched on her toes sometimes, or dipped her too fast, and she yelled at him. My heart broke to keep him from Heidi, but she would have put a stop to things, no matter how much joy I knew the illusions would give her, if she wouldn't get so worried. I guessed, with the hospitals and fellowship, I had seen sides of gladness and vitality that Heidi hadn't. Emma taught me not to be limited by normalcy, and Dr. Walsh said behavior works or doesn't. Since the incident at Heidi's science fair, Tita May had returned to work, and she was winning cases. I would tell Heidi eventually, tomorrow, next week. Anyway, I would keep monitoring the situation.

With Tito back in my life, it was hard to stay grumpy at Tina. He always had a mellowing effect on me, and I'm sure all of his patients, with his eyes, lovely frown, and odd laugh. I wouldn't need deep breathing if he was around. I thought if he had been alive when I went crazy, he would have known what to do, but Tita May and Heidi succeeded on their own. He told me that Tina hadn't meant any harm, that it wasn't right to hold carelessness against a person.

I had been determined not to notice Tina, so I was shocked that she was happier after we started talking again. The music on her speakers changed from country to rap and, as we cemented our relationship again, blues. Her desk became an improvised pantry. She replaced the textbooks

## Chapter 17

with ingredients for her creations, so nobody in the dorm would steal the real food that she biked widely to secure. The effects of this replacement on her grades shunted her on a different life path that would eventually be satisfying. She fed Dan, which gave them something to discuss happily.

At Dan's suggestion, I broke through the creator's block I'd been suffering for my fellowship project. He convinced me it was irrational to worry that others would steal my idea. I started sharing more graphic thoughts in fellowship group, which pleased Emma, since she believed in open source revolution.

"Martha, I cherish watching your soul force echo in these chambers. I think you're becoming an example of the journey that creativity destroys. Will you be the student mentor for next year's fellows?"

I said I needed to think about it. The metal seed glinted in my pocket enthusiastically, and I filled Lolo Junjun's notebook. I used the whiteboard regularly, one day plotting all of our concepts in rings as I had seen Emma draw. The scattered, divergent web scared us. Dev and I uncovered a preconscious theme in our ideas, and he introduced me to his adviser, an emeritus professor specializing in weaponized mud. The professor had fifty years of experience in the field of urban design, and he was still breaking new ground with his latest theory, expansion of urbanism to wooded areas. He trembled, I think with echoing soul force, as I described my project and told me that he, too, thought about the Ardennes Forest of World War Two sometimes. Our ideas parted in that he planned to fill the Ardennes with Russian mud, or *rasputitsa*.

"If mud saved Moscow, it would have saved France," he said.

At first, I realized sadly that we would be in competition, because gold trees couldn't grow in *rasputitsa*. He clarified that he hadn't decided whether he meant to fill the Ardennes literally or symbolically. He became a fun friend I visited often.

Heidi and her adviser kicked around an idea about mirror neurons and empathetic time travel, which would later distinguish Heidi as a lantern of science. She had become bored with what she called her childish research, and she wasn't looking forward to the international science fair, except to see Tucson for the first time. Tita May, who was more excited than Heidi for her trip, asked me to stay with her over spring break while Heidi was gone. I hardly hesitated before agreeing. I congratulated both of us on our enduring stability.

"What took you so long?" Tita May said. "Get to the point! No more nonsense. Hurry up, Martha. You're running out of time!"

# Chapter 18

My eyes open without heaviness since I don't take my pills. It's black outside, and I forgot to remember the day. If I want, I can have the same day tomorrow. The first thing I do when I wake up is read, while the light is still white and thin. I read everything—menus I saved from dinner, sides of boxes, maps that I turn until the compass is upside-down. Any words tighten my writing, until the letters can't be pulled apart. I read and reread as if I created these words, too. The sounds get into my muscles, which feel softer from months of writing in my room. They were soft to start.

I've written enough that I can feel a break in the story after it happens. The cursor winks, and the faces fade along with the screen when I shut it. I'm almost always alone, or it feels that way when I'm in the middle of writing. At the break, I leave the house. I take a walk with my story. By the time I get outside, people start to come into the streets. I learn to tell about people from their coats and hats, and I check my imagination when I follow them into stores for my own errands. I haven't seen a single face twice.

I've seen tomorrow coming from a far distance, felt its shadow like the end of holidays or the tail of a comet. I don't know if I'll see a same day of calm and still writing. The quality and slant of the sun have already changed. My body lets me write when I'm sick and depressed. The pain clears for a minute of sentience and something to say. I'm already changing my mind—it's already healing and refashioning. I'll tell the doctors that the writing is as good as electric. If I keep writing, the blood in my brain will catch the current.

I'll end my story where I want, wherever would have been best. I'll make him paper. I know how. I don't want to know who I'll be, if I wake up and he's gone. I don't see why memories have to distill, lose smallness until they sparkle. I don't want him unclouded. I'd keep every impurity if I could, all the wrinkles and his own forgetfulness. In my book, his memory will ignite, next to mine.

# SPRING QUARTER: ELEGANTLY SPINNING

# Chapter 19

The start of spring break brought out a swagger in me because it really looked like I was going to finish my third freshman year. Grades weren't out yet, but I had a good feeling, the lucid kind of good. Dan found out he'd aced everything, which, unlike other amazements from our first year, turned out to be impressive. Psychology would come precociously to him in undergraduate. He finally met his consuming lifelong challenge, besides me, in graduate school when he'd study therapy. For now, we celebrated ourselves with nachos each, in a dismal bar. We thought this spot had a dirtiness that was almost distinguished in how it made the room darker, more enigmatic. It could have been very old, for California. Other people came to watch games on the anachronistic flatscreens, but we came to talk in the cushioned booths that absorbed every new misunderstanding.

Lying in bed after celebrating, I felt contented, in a humbly-enthralled-with-myself kind of way, that I'd managed to claw from starving depression to the resounding normalcy of my day: restaurants and sex, like they weren't ever hopelessly alien parts of somebody else's life. The thought of the day would have been a movie to me a year ago. I told Dan how I was feeling, and he agreed that I was a

## Chapter 19

very resilient person. Still, he wondered whether I was ready to spend so much time with Tita May over spring break.

If I was honest, it wasn't the dancing that made me nervous as much as her new way of talking. She never left the courtroom anymore, locking into quarrels with Heidi and me like our causes were pathetic, like ordering appetizers represented the dissolution of virtue, in her words. I could see how she was winning every case. I had gotten pretty good at philosophizing from probably passing my classes, and I had to say that every argument was consistent. She was operating under different rules though, for a different world or time, that obeyed our logic but resisted reality. Heidi got mad at Tita May for being unscientific.

I knew we'd probably get into a fight, and I wasn't sure why she asked me to stay with her because I was sure she knew it, too. She talked a lot about how she'd be alone in the house after Heidi moved away, but she never argued with it. Her voice got funereal and ponderous, and she sucked in her cheeks until they caved when we brought it up. The thought of that house, spotless again, was filling with ghosts, she told Heidi and me.

It might end up being an unhappy spring break for both of us, but I had been happy enough lately that I thought I could spare some for Tita May. Dan seemed to think, even if she was showered and working, that some contagion hung around, had drowned the fabric of rooms in micro mud. To be fair, he hadn't seen Tita May since the science fair, but he didn't believe me that she was much better. He said I had been doing so well, hadn't been manic a bit last quarter even with all the drama. Dan said Tita May needed to care for herself, if she really was better, just as I needed to decide whether I wanted to catch whatever berserk cracked under her clean.

"It runs in the family," Dan said. Hearing himself, he stiffened and blinked rapidly, shaking his head. "I didn't mean that. I mean, mental illness runs in families."

He busied himself packing for his flight tomorrow, while I sat on his bed with a comic.

"Dan, I'm not like Tita May. We're different people," I said. I remembered to soften my voice to signal I didn't care about his verbal slip, all this political correctness toward being insane.

Dan put away packing to initiate his active listening. He crossed his legs and nodded, ready to agree. "Grief isn't the same as depression. And trauma is different, too."

"Really? Because it all feels the same to me."

I hated his vocabulary for pain.

"They're actually distinct with overlapping symptoms," Dan said. "But who cares? We always talk in class about how the DSM is rigged anyway."

"I care. What do you mean? Are you saying diagnoses aren't real?" I said. "It means something to me. I'm not making it up." The voice I was hearing sounded dangerous.

"That's not what I meant. I'm agreeing with you, you're different. Sometimes you're really creative. It doesn't mean you're psychotic. She sees things that aren't there, which is really sad. Delusional. She probably has schizophrenia. Worse prognosis. You're not going to be like her. Don't worry. I feel terrible for Heidi. What's she going to do about MIT now? No matter what happens, I'm not going to leave you alone."

I didn't understand why he kept talking while the blood rose to fill my eyes. He swam in front of me in pools of red. When we met, Dan told me he loved the lake picture; he lied. I thought of Tita May's cake and swing-dancing, and all those words smashed from his mouth in bullets.

## Chapter 19

"You don't know anything about us. You think because she likes you that you can talk about her like that? You never saw me until I was fine, and you think this is me. The funny thing is, you still think I'm sick. It'll never be enough. I hate you!"

He absorbed the yelling like it was another whim of mine. "All we talk about is you," Dan said. "You never listen. Now you think you know me?"

The blood sapped out to the floor, and only my suffocated parts remained. "I don't want to know you anymore."

"How can you say that? We're going to be something great. You said so. Let's go to sleep already."

"I don't want you anymore, Dan."

"I never knew why you wanted me anyway. I'm a horrible person. I'm sorry. But I'll be better, make it up to you. We're going to talk it out. I'll listen. You can tell me everything. I won't laugh at you, I promise. Go to sleep, you'll like me again. We'll be fine in the morning. We'll talk in the morning, okay? I won't laugh."

I didn't care what happened next. I grabbed my clothes and pills, threw on pants, and left. The night bit me all over as it took me. I clutched my things to my chest, but they fell apart in my hands. I could have touched his face thinking of how he looked at me first. But the lightning had crackled into static that itself sputtered sparks into nothing. I was sure I had seen us married. Fear of unholy things crept into my guts and chilled them. I guessed I had escaped my future, messed with its order until the crossings exploded. I didn't know what would come out next. I didn't know then, when I would see Dan again. I didn't know him yet.

# Chapter 20

"You already regret it," Tita May said. The pan hissed. She fried *ukoy* for me, a snack after work. I ate the lacy fritters off a paper towel. She had cooked the fridge full with my favorites for the five dinners we'd spend together.

"You will never do better. I've seen it myself, for my own eyes," Tita May said. "He only ever wanted to love you. What did that boy ever do to you?"

"It's not important what he said. Why do you have to know the details of everything?" I said.

My voice was pitchy. I dreaded that she would get it out of me, if she kept bearing down. She only bore down lately. Tita May might have laughed off Dan's words, but I knew her less now.

"Tita May, I'm better without him. You're not going to change my mind. I don't know why you take his side. You don't even know Dan."

"I know enough. I've seen how he looks at you, those eyes," Tita May said. The plate banged on the table after she refilled it.

"Is it because he's a nerd? You're not special yourself. He's the special one. You don't even know him. Who will you be without him now?" She ripped a fritter into pieces.

## Chapter 20

"Is it because you think you're too young? What else are you going to do with your life? It doesn't matter what you collect. Keep going as you are. You'll be alone with nothing but regrets to keep you company. Until the day you die."

"Tita May! Don't be so dark. You're creeping me out," I said. Something squiggled down my spine. Her eyes were burning, crumbling into ashes. "I am too young. We only knew each other for four months. What were you expecting?"

"Tell me again what you told him when you threw him away."

"I don't even remember anymore. It's what I told you before. It was short. Then I left."

"You forget, I remember. You told him you didn't want him anymore," Tita May said. "Martha, really, how can you throw a person away?" I felt as ashamed as when she caught me in a battle with Heidi.

"So careless. So young, fifteen years old, think it can't matter, that you have time to change your mind back and forth and more. Who knows how much life you get? Either of you? When you're my age, you're going to regret what you said with everything left to you. You're going to miss him until you die yourself, too late."

"I'm nineteen, Tita May."

"That's what I said. Don't talk to me with that tone. So hard-headed." She tucked a few fritters into a napkin and went upstairs.

I hardly saw her eat. She cooked, portioned dinner for me and herself in a paper plate, and ate somewhere else. I couldn't ask, and she looked like she didn't have time. She complained that other public defenders complained that minutes weren't enough to prepare clients for trial. When we were able to talk, she'd say she couldn't stand working with dumbos anymore. She absorbed cases in seconds, took on other people's caseloads on top of her own. She didn't remember the last time she lost. When she got home, she labored on a master deep cleaning schedule she put together in her spare research, usually some kind of scrubbing. She tossed sponges after a project. I ran into her when her task took her to the kitchen, where I sat with my fellowship plans after dinners.

"How's your project going anyway?"

I couldn't fit my models onto the table, so I had little to show. She had removed all the food and unplugged the fridge, not to waste fuel while she scoured each surface. She set a timer to re-plug the fridge periodically, shoving the food back into their places, so our meals wouldn't cool to a bacterial temperature. Then she'd unplug again, migrate the food, and resume. The timer kept going off.

"It's going really well. I've got the design down, going to start on the machine work soon. A lot of us are new to building, so they've got us in special classes. We had orientation in the machine shop, but the classes will really get going in spring. The equipment's all new, the best. I'm excited to see it all come together."

"What is the point of it again?"

"It's a monument to war and nature, re-imagining fortified trees in the Ardennes Forest."

"I thought it was an oral history." I couldn't catch her expression because she wouldn't stop moving.

"I was interested in that, but Emma said I still needed to make a tree. And I couldn't figure out how to work it in. Now I'm too far into things to make major changes." I flipped open Lolo Junjun's notebook to show her.

"Martha, are you kidding me?" She leaned on the table, bearing down until her arms stood rigid. "What are you doing with your life?" Her eyes blazed.

## Chapter 20

"I take it you never contacted my friend. You forgot about Arthur. What have you been doing instead? Wasting your days away on frivolity? Too many jokes, like life is all laughs. Is that really how you want to remember yourself? Tell the truth for once. You're running out of time. Get serious. I gave you his phone number at the science fair. He told me he would help you. He's waiting for you, Martha. He's very interested, and now he thinks I lied. You weren't listening, were you. How are you going to build a monument to war without talking to any veterans?"

It was the most we'd talked yet. I looked into her eyes and found nothing. It was all stupid, or harmful, not even silly like I hoped.

"You're right, Tita May. I'm sure he'll have a new perspective. And you're right, war is the common theme. I'll talk to Arthur."

"And when is that going to be? I don't see your phone."

She watched as I pulled my phone out, yelled when I needed his number again, and looked over my shoulder as she dictated the text for me.

"There you go. You'll hear from him soon. Don't forget about Arthur again. You're already late. Hurry up, Martha. He's waiting for you. It's been too long, but he'll remember. You can't avoid him forever. Sooner or later, you have to see him. It'll help, seeing Arthur, even if you're not ready yet. You're running out of time. You need to hurry now, or you'll miss him for good."

When the house had four people, and then three, and I imagined even when it was two, everybody inside heard and had a lot of talk. Tita May usually equalized her affections with her temper, but she stopped talking sometimes, especially when Tito pissed her off. In these times, the rest of us talked to ourselves, but some magnetism was missing, loosening us. We forgot how to relate to each other, or we were afraid of her. She could never hold back for long, though.

I started out waiting for the reunion. But she condensed her cleaning schedule into half the days, worked on her timing to optimize efficiency until I only saw her as a buzzing noise here and there. I thought I was keeping my word to Heidi, and Tita May wasn't my responsibility to break, especially in a few short days. Heidi would manage it when she got back. Until then, the silence helped me work.

Music got me up one morning. Shimmering drums cut the weekday quiet. I guessed Tita May had adjusted her hours, which she sometimes did for evening appointments. The office door was open, and I thought she wanted me to see. I hoped and feared that I would find her dancing. When the house was filthy, they had kept the office spotless, as the rest of the house had become in her recovery.

She was sitting in piles of detritus. Heaps of clothes, in thirty years of colors, gave off a human smell. His hospital scrubs were newly pressed. Half-used soaps and razors with hair were set out before an arrangement of candles. A year of daily newspapers, organized and ironed, sat on the bed according to month. Rings, cuff links, and medals shined. His bottles of holy water were arrayed by height next to his wooden and gold icons, crosses, rosaries. Dead flowers added to the noxious smell. Spotlights ignited the statue.

"Martha, how do you do it? You have to tell me. It's a secret. You can tell me. I thought if I collected his things, it would be enough. You said once it has to be specific. But I think I need more, don't I? What do I need? Tell me."

"Tita May, I don't know how I do it."

"I don't care about being better if it means I lost him. You're the only one who understands."

I told her again.

## Chapter 20

"You don't know how? No, you're right. I don't know how I did it, either. Whatever it was, I've lost him for good. I haven't seen him since I don't remember when. I'm a bad person now. A throw-away person. I needed him."

She wore a foil crown around her head, made of starred tinsel. She tossed her hands, locked the door, and paced her way downstairs. She forgot she still wore the crown.

"I hate this house. Our house," she said. "I'd rather work myself to death than live here. I'll burn it down." The crown winked at me.

"What about Heidi?"

"When Erning leaves, it's pointless. Martha, I know you can figure it out, how you do it. You figured out everything else. I'll get it back, like you did. You can try it now, if you want. I'll observe. Would that help?" She reached to shake my shoulder lightly.

"I can't travel in time anymore. My medicine."

Tita May fell back, not a collapse but a slow drawing from me, curving and then binding her spine, rubbing first her forehead and then her hands together.

"Oh, right. No, you shouldn't. I understand. I'm sorry."

I decided then that I couldn't keep things from Heidi anymore. Tita May returned to her labor, the piles of cases at work and invisible dirt in the house, but things she'd said made my gut worm. I didn't know what to do with the numinous feeling, hated that I judged her, when her lack of judgment had healed me. I told Heidi what I'd seen but in weak conditionals. I needed to be fair to Tita May.

Heidi came through the door rejoicing, flipping her hair in freedom. She placed in the fair, true, but she met someone who had kindled a real idea in her. The conversation was nothing substantial at first, she said, just comparing notes. But then pieces seen and unseen closed together in her mind by magnetism. She called her adviser that same minute.

She hadn't solved it yet, or even plotted it, but the inspiration glowed with breakthrough. She was sure. Her adviser wanted her to begin immediately. She wouldn't have time until summer, and she didn't think she could make it. Her adviser said he would wait for now, but someone could scoop her any day. Did she have to go to class? Heidi spilled out her victory over snacks and cake, still wearing her coat since she'd skipped the closet to find her mother faster.

"My god, Erning, nothing can stop you," Tita May said.

"I missed you, Ma. So much. How were things at home?"

"The house is fine. Work is fine. Martha kept me company, don't worry. You work hard, *anak*. You'll make discoveries, so don't think about me. Distracting. You don't have time to waste anymore, my dear. You're going to burn down everything."

"Ma, what are you talking about?"

"I want you to get what you want, all of it."

# Chapter 21

I was young and hadn't seen a life fall apart up close, except mine. I heard about them: luminous, vital people embittering into dust after disaster. But I didn't know their secrets. I thought I'd see them at reunions or someplace, like how movies showed people made wrong choices. Tita May always had many sides to her, and I heard from Heidi about Tita May's occasional wrath. They never fought about meaningful things. In the matters that counted, Tita May was as immovable and reliable as a monument. We thought it made sense that someone so full of ardor should overflow now and then. There was nothing to forgive, because her love expressed itself even in the anger, how bound she was to our lives.

I started to suspect that it wasn't another tantrum, that her life was really ruined. She didn't burn anymore; her rage wasn't of the earth or anything to do with us. The way her eyes rested, it seemed she could lose us without a whimper. It could be that her personality had fundamentally changed, and she was lost to us as she said Tito was to her. I realized how long life was, that we might have to call on our memories of her to keep loving.

I tried to remember that I had other reasons to break up

with Dan. I hated that the despair, breaking over me in barbs, could prove he was right about us. I told myself it didn't have anything to do with her, or at least not only her and me. The real problem was that I spent my days breaking things.

At first, I blamed distractions. It had been an intense spring break and quarter. I hadn't been at school or outdoors this long since I was seventeen. My legs hurt at the end of the day. Everyone else said they were stressed and burned out.

Building was new to me. Everybody caught on faster, but I refused to think I was worse than them. I'd persist, like I used to. I spent longer and longer nights breaking things. The planes never lined up, the holes were off by a hair, the metal melted at the wrong angles, by a couple degrees. It didn't matter how close I got. Things broke at the ends of things anyway. They were junk, didn't care that I had almost executed. I counted on it. My hands grew welts that popped. Everybody else's projects reached higher and higher. I watched them climb, spires in all directions. I almost closed in sometimes, measured it all to exactness, and then the mess would tip over and crash. It wouldn't stop clattering. The noise was humiliating.

Nobody had time. I couldn't pay anyone to do it, because what could I say I had done if I did? The last exit congested over, because I had almost run out of money, and I calculated barely enough materials to finish. I saw my tree shrink smaller and smaller, until it was the size of the foil model I had created out of so much triumph.

I skipped classes in order to break things. When I went, I was failing. I didn't see how I could finish. I lied to Tina about my progress, faked radiance whenever we saw each other. We both had long days.

More than anything, I hated the feelings of things destroying themselves in my hands. I saw the metal drip and

## Chapter 21

snap. I heard and felt whip cracks when it did. I didn't have anywhere to go besides the machine shop. It fogged over in my mind and then my vision, the lathes and saws darkly irresistible. I returned to an old idea, and it met me warmly. I realized, with some delight, that I had wormed it inside the whole time. Something I hadn't lost. But its glow was gone. The lake told me no, and I couldn't go back to try another path. I tried many times. The lake knew better. The thought of killing myself tired itself out. Another exit sealed.

A better idea was to cut everything off from the start. If I hadn't been born, I wouldn't need to forget my pain, because nothing at all existed. Or would I become a brain in a jar? The logic dawned, a creeping sun. I started preparing for my trip, packing food for myself and the baby. In the movies, people exploded when they met their past selves, and I would be fine with that, too. I would take the baby away. In time, the plans germinated some kind of forward-going in me. I would take the baby. We would live someplace together, alone. I would figure out from there. I stopped going to machine shop, stopped breaking things, in order to plan. Hope came back with a drunk anesthesia. I would raise the baby myself. We would grow old together, the two of us until we broke, and the baby would fix me before I died. The circle would close. It was gorgeous.

The baby was just too ugly. I had gone back too early. It was a man's wrinkled bump, with pouches all over. The smell, yeasty in the air, made me sick. I gave up.

I had tried everything. I wondered dumbly if I should go to the hospital. Or call Dr. Walsh. But I didn't see myself doing it, getting on my bike or picking up the phone. I started eating more, then faster, then slower. I sat in the corner of the machine shop watching all the people. I watched for days, all the hours, taking notes in Lolo Junjun's notebook. I sat in class watching all the people. People looked scared, but everything was scared of me. Even Tina.

With a thump of inspiration, I remembered the powers I had earned. I watched myself breaking things and laughed from a far distance. The tree was junk. How could I forget? War was junk anyway. I wondered if this could be the symbolism. My depression had led me to war. It fit. I told Emma all about it. The symbol would guide my creator's hands. She asked if I was sleeping. She told me to talk to humans. Things only symbolized humanity, she said. Where could I find a human? Thump! I laughed. I watch myself from a far distance showing up at Arthur's house. I hope I'm not too late.

Behind the screen, the door was open. The music was too loud. I recognized it, from long ago, some kind of jazz. But it was the bad kind, composed, no spontaneity. All chords rising and falling. A very old man turned a corner, and all the horns blared. His face wasn't pouches. It was almost smooth. His house smelled of bread.

"Who's there? How did you get in? Who are you?"

"You left the door open. I'm Martha."

"Martha Marcelo? May's niece. Was our appointment today? Forgive my memory. I thought I wrote it down. Must have missed it. Darn. Come, come."

His carpet was shagged with some kind of caterpillar, but I walked across anyway. Quick. He sat me down into a couch as orange as burning. Bad jazz gave me an earache. I treasured the pain as it dulled and ascended. Arthur sat across from me, in a chair made of straw, and I met his eyes.

"I have waited for you, Martha. It has been too long. But I am glad you are here finally. You are not too late. I will never forget you. You are here now. I was pleased to get your message. Time to talk."

## Chapter 21

He served me chocolate milk and a cookie that crunched like cartilage. I remembered he didn't know what he was asking of me. I pulled out Lolo Junjun's notebook, read the bookmarked questions I practiced with Emma. Optimize.

"Thank you for talking to me. It's the Bond-Rummy Fellowship."

"Of course, Martha. It is my pleasure."

"Where are you from?"

My voice was sliding out too fast from its inside lips, but I'd push until my eyes watered. I was hearing him faster than his outside lips could move, scrawling his answers in perfect shorthand, flipping pages until they ripped out. Crispy.

"I am an American citizen. My family remains in Baguio. Where are you from?"

"Manila. When did you join the army?"

"What? Who told you that? I have never been in the army. My brother was in the army. Alvin, never me. I was in the resistance, the guerrilla."

"How old were you?"

"When? I am eighty-one last month. The year was 1943. That makes me sixteen. No, fourteen? How old are you?"

"Nineteen. Why did you join?"

"So many questions. The guerrilla fighters helped my family."

"What was a day in your life?"

"What? I was a young man. I could not leave my family. When the guerrilla wanted, I came. I am very fast. Okay. Are you ready now? I do not have much time. I forgot you were coming."

The final exit banged off.

"Our mission was victorious," Arthur said. "You must understand. Are we finished with questions?"

"Sure. Nice to meet you, Arthur." I was falling away.

"It is nice to meet you, Martha. We will talk more afterwards." He settled into his chair until his bald head made holes in the cushion. I put my bag back on the floor.

"Now, May informed me it is an art project," Arthur said.

"Yes. It's a showcase," I said. He was listening now. His eyes gleamed, not with impatience. Some buried human interest agitated in me. "You're invited, Arthur. You can see it."

He shook his head. "I would think May told you. Never mind, your *tita* talks too much. No time for listening. I am an artist. I work in silver when I can. Otherwise any metal."

I didn't have time to open the exits. I rooted through them with my nails and scrambled out.

"I thought it was my purpose here. Your *tita* did not tell you I wanted to help? Never mind, I told her months ago. She forgot already." He sighed deeply. "Although, I appreciate the small talk earlier. Come, come."

I tracked his steps as we weaved around spiky chairs, kicking away bugs. He unhooked a door to outside. Its opening edge released dust.

The garage, before he booted up the lights, sent out some dewy taste. My feet picked around shadows. It was humid in the center, endless as a jungle. Arthur clicked the lights. I saw wings and mechanical breeze. Metals of all warmth and quality, glass in motion. Enough gold to live on. I saw Arthur and me mirrored in surfaces curved and smooth. Our faces looked out from every kind of fruit, animal, alive thing. I touched a perfect mango, waving palm, sea. The ceiling had stars and sun. Birds swung and shined on wheels. I'd dig a hole, plant the seed in my pocket into platinum earth.

"I understand you will make a tree. A difficult project. Unfortunately, I no longer have adequate equipment. My best work is from the Philippines." He picked up an elephant

## Chapter 21

rider.

"We can use the machine shop. It has everything." He would give me everything.

"I warn you, Martha, I have not made anything in a long time."

Arthur never lied. He'd forgotten some of metalworking, but he held onto great swaths that unfolded easily. Whatever he forgot was soon forgotten itself, because he remembered faster than I listened or ever learned. When he forgot, he chirped out into the shop, and anybody came running to help him. He clapped us on the back for a reward, and whoever it was laughed the rest of the day. Even when he wasn't saying much, he told us stories, because his faces at whatever unraveled were witty as anything. Things never broke. Or if they did, he knew and came to me.

We were building roots and then trunk, chopping and coiling metal, when Arthur told me my favorite story. Alvin was hidden in the tree. Arthur searched, climbed, Alvin jumped, and Arthur broke.

"Smash! The worst was my bones. I could hear them crack and then snap! I wanted to rip off my own ears. So much red, my god. The most I saw up to then. My head was bursting! I thought I broke it, too. I screamed so loud, I made him turn around. He ran back and had to carry me to the hospital. Running the whole way! He was so sorry, he visited me every day. Never missed one day."

Arthur trimmed the treetop again and again.

Some stories we recognize right away. Their words flicker oddly in the mind, like glimpses of things we shed or invented or will. When we hear them again, it feels like a final joining. Arthur's story hit me this way. Past my layers of slush, something about the breaking or blood or reunion. Arthur speaks slowly, so I almost caught each word as it fell. He repeated it every time I asked.

"Nothing but screaming! Noisy. The animals even ran away from us! But Alvin could outrun them as well."

I started to write the words inside my mind, saw the shapes talking to me again. I watched the story grow. We ourselves climbed higher into our silver tree. Every afternoon before we began, I walked for a ladder, then a taller and taller one. Arthur welded and twisted the leaves around the branches. I lifted a basket of leaves, which he dipped into, until I had to refill. His fingers moved with instinct in their joints, and he chatted away while the tree grew.

"I know the trees and hills of Baguio better than my own finger. I could not forget them if I tried to erase. My mother tells everyone, I followed Alvin before I could talk. We are always playing in the hills. He showed me every leaf. And I taught the guerrilla."

He taught me now. We rolled, traced, veined, pressed, fired. I heaped baskets with leaves. Soon, I could make leaves while looking for him, as he formed the curvature of branch after branch, as smoothly as if the tree spun on a great wheel. He prattled on in a slow, inevitable tone.

"I think I am fast, but, I am telling you, Martha, he beat me. He was the strongest in our *barangay*. Our village. I do not believe them that he could die on his feet."

We would run out. I couldn't let Arthur pay for more metal, so I sponged around, sold some things. I wouldn't sell the lake picture. Tina showed me an ad, soliciting copy editors for the local paper. I didn't have any time, but Tina said I could edit from anywhere anytime. I heard her say I was a great writer. After I got back from shop each night, I opened the latest story and read the words again and again until they became sounds. I listened to my ear. Along with the stories, the punctuation healed me, every dot until I could

## Chapter 21

say what I thought again.

"I love the newspaper, Arthur. The time flies by. And I think I'll be able to write for the rest of my life. Whenever I think I lost it, it comes back. The editor says I'm good. Really good, she said. She has to let me write, especially if I get the internship. I just need to find a good enough story for my application."

"Write the story of Alvin. I have always wanted more people to hear what he did, the kind of man he was."

"Arthur, that's perfect. Thank you. Let's do it."

We sat under our silver tree. If I remember where it went, I find us sitting there. Sometimes facing each other, other times shoulder to shoulder, his laugh a barking noise. I realized I like hearing the same stories again and again, even prefer it that way. Years later, I'd forget almost all of it, but I feel the wind from rushing trains, doors sliding open, jumping inside to the city. Doors closing. He never forgot me.

It was one of the best chapters of my life until Heidi called. It still is.

# Chapter 22

Tita May sobbed all day. She said she did everything wrong, that she shouldn't have gone to EDSA, she should have stayed with him in the hospital instead. She didn't recognize him. She was only a child—how could she have known? They ran out of time, and she wanted all of it back. He never forgave her. She saw it in his eyes. Maybe he would have lived if she stayed. Maybe she killed his heart from the start. If she said yes, they could have had more years. More children. Heidi would not have been an only child. Except for Martha. Which one would she choose? She didn't know which would forgive. She should have given up on him long ago and started over. Hadn't she known, in her heart of hearts, that he was lost? Why did she keep looking? She had chosen the dead over the living, and now the living had died, too. She paced from the bed to Tito's sculpture and back again.

"I can't follow her at all," Heidi said. "I think it's delusions now. I'm really worried, Martha. We can't stay with her all day. Should we put her in the hospital?"

"I don't know. She's going to hate it there. Maybe she'll be better tomorrow. We can wait another day."

We tried to sleep in Heidi's bed. Tita May refused to leave the door open, but we woke up periodically to listen and check. She was silent much of the time or working neatly on the sculpture. She cleaned her hands. Heidi returned to bed, and I pretended to be asleep to reassure her that I was resting. But I was awake and smiled to hear fewer tears. In the morning, Tita May ate breakfast downstairs, and Heidi's face lost wrinkles. After we washed up, we heard her yelling at Tito.

"We didn't both have to clean," Heidi said. "Why didn't we split up? We're so stupid!"

We raced up the old stairs. Tita May addressed the statue, now becoming red with temper, other times demanding absolution. She told Tito that he didn't understand, that he had no right to judge her or anybody. He didn't know more just because he died first. It wasn't her fault that he had been such a loser, pursuing a child. Why didn't he court her properly from the start? Why was love always the woman's responsibility? If she hadn't been facing a statue, I would have thought we were children again interrupting an adult spat.

"Heidi, she might not be mad," I said.

"What are you saying? Martha, are you seeing what's happening?"

"We weren't there. We don't know what happened."

"She's not making any sense. It's getting worse. I'm trying to listen, and she's talking in circles, all around the day she met Dad, the revolution. Wait, it's true. No, we don't know anything for certain. We weren't there. That's right. We can't know unless you go back. Maybe she isn't mad. You could find out. Then she'll talk to me again." Her voice dawned with the logic she cherished. Heidi wanted the logic to make her hope true, so she insisted.

She knew I couldn't travel without giving up my medicine. I choked down the resentment that tasted like backed-up bile. I was ashamed of it. We heard Tita May murmuring through the door. She had loved me back into sanity, and now I wouldn't give up any for her peace. Terror stole in because I feared meeting even Tito's incomplete image in the sculpture. Death had given him clarity about the living; he knew everything now. He wouldn't forgive me for skipping his funeral, for laying him aside without ceremony. If I met him again, I'd see his eyes had changed. He would love me less than I remembered and as much as I deserved in life.

It had been my shift for sleep, and I woke up to relieve Heidi. She sat on the floor at Tita May's bedside, and they argued in hoarse whispers. Heidi and Tita May jumped at the opening door, and they scowled at me for the disturbance, with shining eyes shut to me and everything outside.

"I know she wants you to go. You won't have to do anything. Find my parents. Pay attention, listen to everything, take notes. I'll figure it out like I always do. I'll work harder, I'll fix it. I can solve it, and I'll bring her back to me. Otherwise, what was the point of everything else? I did everything for my parents, and now I've lost both of them. Then she'll listen. She'll talk to me again. I miss her so much. She asked me to forgive her for throwing Dad away. Don't you want to know what happened? I have to know! I've never asked you for anything, Martha."

I slept easier in my own bed that night. My professor wouldn't let me skip the exam. I'd do poorly anyway, but I was guilty for my relief that I could leave, grateful for the empty buses. The statue had given Tita May sufficient answer for a while, and she slept for the first time in days. Heidi slept, too. I hoped they would sleep for weeks. I ate with Tina in the dining hall, relishing our own easiness, which hadn't diminished for good after all. Stanford never looked so lovely as those days, evergreen and red roofs, a retreat bounded

## CHAPTER 22

from any waiting ugliness. Life here was biking downhill, when I only had to roll past palms and books for joy beyond fading or death. I was a fool to think it had ever been hard. Heidi called to say that Tita May hadn't been admitted to the hospital. Heidi wasn't allowed in the intake room. She said Tita May must have lied to the doctors. Not on purpose, Heidi cried. None of it touched me because my gravity was reversing back to the sun; I was drifting and then floating, cord cut, loosened, following currents now upstream and downstream.

"You stopped taking your medicine," Tina said.

She brought me a dinner tray. I didn't bristle because I had been waiting for her to notice. It wasn't too late to throw the pills back again, forsake the people I loved for a grounded life. I was still close, hovering but my toes almost touched, if I tried. I used to think the stable life was the worthwhile one, but I'd forgotten the intoxication, the generosity of my illusions. Was I a better person when I was sane? I had been waiting for Tina to notice. I relied on her to tell me what she thought. I wasn't sure if I'd agree, but I needed somebody I could trust.

She listened as she always would. But she said nothing for once, running her hands over her candle that she never lit.

"Do you remember when I missed our first day? And you told me nobody could tell? I said I had to drive my mom and dad back. I wouldn't let them behind the wheel. Because they'll say they're dry, they'll go to meetings, and then they'll show up to my first day of college with booze hidden in their trunk. I'm that dumb, I thought they were proud of me. Martha, you don't know how lucky you are to have her." She turned to me, eyes lit with begging.

"Why do you hate them so much?"

Her face broke.

"I don't hate my parents. Why would you say that? I'd do anything for them if I could stand them. We can't count on them for anything. Victor acts like nothing happened, but I won't. I'm not going to forget what they did. You try really hard to be happy. They used to try harder, like you. I didn't forget. You know me. I try to be nice, but I'm not like you. They don't want to try anymore, so they drink. They gave up. Look, Martha, you're not like them. You'd be better if you could. You don't hurt people. You're not going to give up."

I stopped listening. I touched the metal seed I carried everywhere. "You're the one who gave up," I said. "Everybody's like everybody else. Nobody knows what I'll do."

"You have to do something. She's your mother."

# Chapter 23

Tita May was looking for me. The smells of spicy fur, flood, astringent soap, and incense mixed everywhere. I was in Tito's office, I was hugging Tita May, I was ripping open packages from my unseen family, I was nine years old at the airport where the sticky, steaming humidity stained my last memory of the Philippines.

"My god, I'm sorry. I thought you were my sister. It's so dark. Where is everyone coming from?"

For the shadows themselves were moving. Everywhere an eye could count people were converging. The shortwaves called them into the streets, until every footfall was echoed ten, a hundred times. The rattling of gates as they opened and slammed was the noise of whatever history would be broken that night. Time itself was converging; the still living followed their lost friends into the revolution.

"I heard one of the announcers on the radio. I'm sure it was him. I know his voice anywhere. He said to come. If he's anywhere near Manila, he'll go to EDSA. I'll find him."

We joined the fraying, perspiring crowd. We kicked aside broken bottles and detritus in our path. There was no way to get lost because the people led us where we needed to go.

"My sister's not getting these," Tita May said. "I made

them for the soldiers. He said they're our friends now. I'll protect them if he wants me to." Her backpack was full of sandwiches. Lolo Junjun had told her on the radio that parts of the military defected tonight.

She walked into my mother's improvised hospital and made a face at her sister. I waited at the door. My mother was organizing red, yellow, green, and black ribbons. They were tags for the casualties, and she wouldn't use any. My mother threw up her hands, pointing at the door, when she saw Tita May. Tita May gave her a couple sandwiches from her stock.

I wasn't the only one to see a man lift his head across the hospital floor. His eyes were guided to Tita May by a glittering spotlight. He tripped along the dance pattern, footprints of dripping gold, that spiraled from her feet. The man had Heidi's kind eyes and probably Heidi's gentle voice, if I could have heard him from the door. He tapped Tita May on the shoulder, hands trembling, and she shook him off.

"Who was that guy?" I said, struggling to keep up with her.

"My sister's classmate. He wants to date me if he makes it through the night. He says. Dramatic."

He makes it, I wanted to tell her. He looks at you that way for the rest of his life. Over the dinner table, across transpacific aisles, through your daughter's hair. You'll walk into rooms together for twenty-five years, as long as he makes it. More years than you've been alive. Everyone will look your way, to admire and envy, even after you've lost your beauty together and only the electricity remains. When you walk out, the room is darker.

"He thinks he's so smart because he's the youngest in their school's history. Who cares about history? Why's he in a rush anyway? He doesn't know me yet. My sister says he's the biggest nerd in history. She thinks I'm at home making

## Chapter 23

sandwiches. We're going to Camp Crame."

Everyone was going to Camp Crame. People yelled our purpose, while others padded, pushed, marched, limped on. Tita May and I were strangers and didn't talk much. The gathering thunder was enough to hear. On the way, she yelled at friends when we passed them. Their returning yells tolled in the air, victorious and afraid.

"We must have missed him. He's always moving, he can't stop moving."

Tita May pressed through the crowd of clinging shirts, wet with sweat and steam. We crumpled leaflets of her uncle's face into hundreds of brown hands. We screamed her uncle's name, but his name was buried in the other cheers and screams. Other names. They screamed that the loyalist army was coming for the defectors.

"I can't leave. He's here. He's always in the middle of the action. This is his life. He wouldn't miss it. He's a writer, he wants to tell everyone the story later. He has to tell everyone what happened."

The people joined and planted their bodies, roots scrabbling deeper until they touched tombs. If you looked from the sun, the earth had become brown faces, all turned the same direction: the tanks. "Stand your ground!" I saw the distant army close in on this great, unbent forest. Its front lines hardened, the tanks revved and refused. The people still lasted. They were more powerful than bombshells, as strong and ancient as a trunk of a million rings. In this minute, its growth was eternal. The masses gleamed like gold, lines to the sky. All around Tita May was Lolo Junjun, for she had lifted the yellow leaflets high and dropped every one, his faces circling where she stood her ground. The voices on the radio died and were resurrected. The future president arrived. It was the lady who had tied the yellow ribbons, and her inauguration was tomorrow.

"Ernesto Marcelo! Junjun Marcelo!" Tita May's scream was quieter, worn from days of searching. She had climbed another fence and flagged both arms. People shushed her for interrupting the president's speech.

"Excuse me, Junjun Marcelo? The journalist?" A nun peered into our faces. Her own face past the white habit was dirty, from three days of kicking up road dust and rosaries. The crowds crushed our bodies into each other. She almost dropped her picket sign, and Tita May cleared her hurting throat.

"He's my *ninong*. Have you seen him?"

The nun pulled us close into her heavy dress. I don't know how she survived the heat on the front lines. Her eyes burned as she embraced us. With our heads on her chest, her voice shot straight out of her heart.

"Oh, my darlings. I'm so sorry. I can't believe you haven't been told. Nobody has seen Junjun in almost two years. Listen to me, girls. I had the privilege to write with your *ninong* at the *Collegian*. And everyone will tell you the same. It will all come out. Junjun Marcelo is...he was a hero. Soon, everyone will know."

Next to mine, Tita May's face listened. She would tell everyone what happened. I heard the nun yell at her friends after I pulled away. *"Siya ang pamangkin ni Junjun!"* His name called them into the streets. More humanity crushed into Tita May, and they told her all she would ever know.

"He would have gone. And now I was there," Tita May said. She said she would wait for him—plenty of people would come out of hiding now.

# Chapter 24

"Heidi, the revolution isn't a story," I said. "We'll never know. We weren't there. And we didn't listen, not really. It's our parents' story. We have to get our own. We're too old now."

"I can never do what they did," Heidi said.

"You would have done it," I said. "I saw you." I didn't know about myself.

I used to take it for granted that I would have gone to EDSA, that being born to a brave line made me courageous, even as their hot blood mixed with my one bloodless, nervous life. I was almost as old, then as old, then older than my parents had been when they went. I lost convictions, got new ones, lost those. If cut down, my blood that ran out could only be a dilution, cooler and paler by now. Then I think of Heidi, and my blood gets hot. If someone hurt her, I wouldn't have a choice.

Heidi and I would tell Tita May that we understood. Then her eyes would calm. She wouldn't choke with panic when she saw our faces. She'd recognize how she loved us, how she never gave us up.

"She'll talk to me again," Heidi said.

We found her in bed with her eyes open. She demanded to know, and we tried to make our eyes large with loving. I want to say that she believed us that we believed her. She cross-examined us again and again. I found the events slippery. She caught us in our inconsistencies until we had to remind each other that we weren't lying. But she was making sense. Or she always was.

"She's talking to me again," Heidi said.

Sometimes Tita May laughed. We couldn't find the source, but we saw it was a joyful sound and laughed with her. Heidi and I swore we wouldn't keep things from each other anymore. We planned. Tita May hated all of our plans. She came up with her own, and Heidi and I squirmed around. Sometimes we did talk behind her back, couldn't find a way around it, guiltily promised we'd tell unknown people her secrets if we had to. She didn't believe us that we didn't want to. She got out of bed and painted all day, sometimes the ceiling and once the stove. Fiery brushstrokes licked the walls; she burned everything down.

Tita May became curious, at first warily, about what happened to people she used to know. She wanted to know their movements, whether they were plotting or honest. One day she showed up to work, and she told everyone she would disappear. She told them her blood burned her skin from the inside. We didn't know what was going to happen. We tried to stop her from her plans sometimes, but she wouldn't stop moving. We weren't scared of her anymore. We had seen she was braver in her life than we would ever be.

Some passed her tests, and others weighed worthless. She shared her findings with us, her decisions on who she would keep around. She asked what we thought about her judgments, whether we had any suspects to add. She started holding onto a few people, recalling inch by inch the old trusts of her life.

And one day, she loved us again. Or she always had.

## Chapter 24

Heidi always wants to do more for Tita May. For example, she would use some of her genius grant to buy Tita May a new car. I didn't understand the ethics of it, but she said the money specifically came without strings. That year, my third freshman year, Heidi came into a significant chunk of income for the first time. She won a thousand dollars at the international science fair. Heidi mostly has simple tastes, but she used some of the money to buy the latest video game console. It came out that same month, and she wouldn't stop talking about how it was a miracle. She never talks about miracles. I don't know how she had time for video games, since she always fretted about how she didn't have time for her breakthrough until summer. But she still says it was the best money she ever spent, except for the tickets for Tita May.

I think it's safe to say that Heidi and Tita May are mostly unlike, except for the hard-headedness of their ideas. I've never been like them in that way. I labor to form any opinions. When I do, I worry, because I feel like I'm going to regret them later. Heidi didn't give me time to get an opinion on her newest idea to do more for Tita May.

Heidi's ideas, like her scientific inventions, come out as full bodies, with the force of revelation. Her conviction impresses many people because people like to believe in stuff. They like to believe that somebody believes in something. She decided to buy Tita May tickets to the Philippines, for the Marcelo family reunion that summer. The idea gave me vertigo, and I wanted to fall off my chair. It was true that Tita May had been seeing friends again, including a new doctor.

"I don't know why you keep going to Dr. Walsh," Tita May said. "You know that she's a total amateur, right? Barely out of school. I was not impressed."

Over the next years, she kept at me about Dr. Walsh, and I wondered if her new friend was paying her to advertise. I thought her doctor had strange opinions sometimes. But Tita May was excited about another person, and we thought the interest was good. She met with other friends, and she said she was making new ones sometimes, too.

"She always says she misses her cousins, her godparents, her grandma," Heidi said. "The old house. You remember all the stories, right? Just think, Martha. It makes perfect sense."

I really would be glad if I was wrong, but I knew that the last thing I'd want in my recovery was to see a bunch of old faces. I avoid all the faces I can't absolutely trust, and some are too old to be sure about.

"You and Ma are different people, Martha. Since when has my mother ever been shy? It would be the finishing touch to bring her back. Believe me. You can't treat her like she's sick for the rest of her life." Heidi swung her legs from Tina's top bunk emphatically.

Arthur liked to sit on the bean bag, in spite of our caution about his bad back. "It is a very good idea. Respect for parents is essential. You are returning her sacrifice."

"Exactly. She said she needs a vacation," Heidi said. "She keeps saying that she's alone here. She's been talking about the reunion for years. And she's well enough I think. She'll get even better before the trip. It's weeks from now. Can't you imagine how excited she'll be? I'll email the *lolas*."

Heidi usually convinces me, but I like to try at least.

"What do you think, Tina?" I said. She said she was studying, but she looked at food blogs.

"We don't have many summers left anyway," Tina said. "Victor and I are going on a road trip with my parents. Who knows? I'll rent a getaway car. Martha, you're my ride or die." I promised.

I really wanted to hope, so I pitched in my copy editing

## Chapter 24

savings. Heidi spoke with the *lolas* and planned to reserve dinner at Tita May's favorite restaurant and a stay at some kind of spa or something.

"She loves getting her nails done," Heidi said.

She wasn't sure about the rest of the itinerary yet; she wanted to schedule some free time. Heidi said everyone was excited Tita May was coming. Tita May was everyone's favorite. She said so our whole lives. I kept at the copy editing to chip in for more happiness for Tita May.

Arthur sold a piece to contribute a bit, too, because Tita May was his favorite also. Arthur and I met our first deadline for the tree, even found time to add some fruits. I was happy to have a second deadline lined up for my internship application, but I trusted we'd keep our weekly chats, even if we had all the time in the world. I wasn't sure if he always left the inner door open, but he didn't listen to me about shutting it now and then at least.

"You wouldn't have to lock it," I said. "You can see it's open from the street, Arthur. Anybody could walk in. You wouldn't hear them until they got inside. Especially with your loud jazz all the time."

He didn't care. He brought out a round tin of butter cookies that we couldn't get enough of. We caught up on the last week over hundreds of cookies, planned, sometimes sat around silent but for the chewing. Then I pulled out Lolo Junjun's notebook, and Arthur hummed in his throat.

He told the story with extra spirit, even polish. He didn't leave out a single smashing or crunching this time, added more wildlife and trees, sticks that scraped his face like branching knives, which leaves fell when the toe of his crushed foot brushed. Described the heaviness of the hospital doors, his bed that kicked back and up, the doctor's blaming face, the presents Alvin gave when he visited.

"Because he was so sorry," Arthur said.

"I love this story," I said. "What else, Arthur?" I couldn't stop smiling. I didn't need to write down a thing. It had imprinted, as it was for him.

"Martha, I do not remember anything else."

His face, too often unreadable with its straight, unmoving brows, settled into somewhere peaceful. "Come, come."

I strained slightly to keep up with him, as he sprang up from the table and wound us around the stairs, creaking down loose floorboards with his slippers, until he opened the door to his bedroom. He made a beeline for his bedside cabinet, crouched, almost slid on the ground, wrinkling his ironed pants. He showed me piles of notebooks. They were stacked with their pages facing us, the flat ends of papers in every shade of white.

"As long as you can read, Martha, you will remember everyone. Do not forget. In fact, write it down."

I pulled out Lolo Junjun's notebook, which he examined and approved of, watching to make sure I recorded correctly. He selected the right years.

I followed him into the living room and sat into a stiff-backed, tufted sofa. "More comfortable," he said. He opened the first book, leafed aside a page of vellum along its spiral side coil. His handwriting was looser then. It had tightened up over the years, or at least in the diagrams we made together now. We began to read, and the books told us all we would ever know.

It was at one of these readings that we decided on a last-minute addition to our tree. Emma said she definitively dug the idea and would make an exception for our installation. I drew a mock-up for the design. Arthur thought that I could handle things myself. He left me on my own.

"You are graduating now," he said. "Do you remember

# Chapter 24

what I taught you? Check your book if you forgot. I will tell you our story again and again. You are grown now, Martha. I love you always, no matter what you decide. Do not forget."

I promised.

It was our last unbroken piece of metal, and I'd given all my money toward Tita May. It was impossible that my hand wouldn't shake, but I hoped it would give the plaque an artisanal feel. And anyway, I would shine it up bright. I etched large, so Tita May would be able to read my handwriting. I read each letter's line over and over again, reforming each into my best calligraphy.

"Kuya Alvin Santos. Lolo Junjun Marcelo," she'll read. Then she'll look at me, her hands and hair full of leaves that we'll climb high to pick off. The silver matches the white shine in her hair near the stars.

"You're like him, Martha. You know that? Your energy, your imagination. You feel everything. You're like us. You won't stop moving, will you?"

I'll shake my head, and she'll get better.

She did come and read. She wandered away to the other exhibits, and I followed her. We walked past busted accordions, mud that suctioned in appendages, and a tiny baby turtle. She examined the old and new flags of the Philippines. Tita May has a lot of tolerance for imagination, but I couldn't get a read on what she thought of all this, what we were doing with our lives.

"Tita May, I'm going to do something with my life," I said. "I love stories and people. I'm going to be a journalist. It doesn't matter if I get the internship."

Tita May closed her eyes, pulled me into her hair, and she must have smiled.

After Tita May, the only person left to tell was Emma. She led a group of high school students around the showcase, wearing her most googly purple glasses. She waved a sunflower to point out details. The students stared. Even adolescents were astonished by her. What kind of adult is this?

"Don't forget, boys and girls, symbolism is humanity. For what is a symbol but life's expression of itself? And man is the only life we truly know. Yet."

I thanked Emma for everything, for the tree and for Arthur. I used to feel she picked me by mistake, but I didn't think so anymore. I told her I couldn't be the student mentor because I needed to spend more time at the paper. I waited for her eyes to cast down behind the goggles, but they turned into happy crescents.

"I want you to know, my dear," Emma said. "I was so lucky to have you. Your moods are your flame, and I know they will bring you inspiration, no matter what you do. Don't let them take your madness from you. Keep feeling. And tweet me sometime."

I couldn't guess when she'd known. I promised.

My life was so full at the showcase that I noticed who was missing, but I felt no loss and only excitement to tell her everything. I already heard through the door that she wasn't alone. Part of me saddened that she skipped my moment to hang out with somebody else, but I had to tell her everything anyway.

"Martha, I can't believe we missed your showcase," Tina said. "It wasn't my fault. Tell her what happened."

"Don't look at me."

Victor rested against the window, as much a fixture of my freshman year as the changed sun through the glass. I remembered his hospitality at our first meeting, and he looked friendlier than I thought possible for a stranger. But I replayed our days together and judged that he was my friend.

## Chapter 24

"Ask this one how she missed the exit," Victor said.

Tina laughed until her gums stuck to her lips, and she had to run her tongue over to speak and smile properly. "He's lying, Martha."

"Tina, who cares about you?" Victor hugged me. I breathed in new mist from a river at its source.

"I want to hear about freshman year," he said. "Not you, Tina."

The three of us walked down the hall and into the breezeway where we had begun.

"Victor, you're not going to believe it," I said.

I told him everything that happened after woo-bee woo, more choices that created themselves after I agreed to the one before, how things had rolled and converged and branched. Tina corrected me now and then, and I let her since she was always there after all. Victor made me laugh at how silly it had all been. He was right, and it hadn't taken long for all things to become beloved like he'd said.

Things looked more beloved because Victor was moving to Palo Alto. He got a job at a tech start-up to help people find other people who wanted to work on a start-up. It was an app.

"They say it's supposed to bring people together across boundaries and privacy," Victor said. "I'm quitting as soon as I find a music gig. Co-workers are nice, though. Nobody cares if I store all my instruments in the innovation open mind plan concept creator place. They're going to get those human hamster balls for the Grand Lawn next. They've been saying that for a while, though. You go to work whenever you want. I'll probably go in a couple days."

He would work at the company until he successfully pitched his concept for a jazz club to his boss, who funded his musical experiments as long as he performed in the company's concert hall every month.

"I heard you tried some improvisation," Victor said. "You left it out of the story. I don't know if you knew this, Martha, but improvisation doesn't mean don't practice." I checked, but his eyes looked merry, and Tina bent over laughing. I smiled because her hair bobbed up and down.

"I don't know what Tina told you, but that was a long time ago," I said. "I quit Voices of Reason last quarter, so it was my last show. The grand finale." He laughed at my joke like he always would.

"So you're available then?" Victor said. "I'm starting a jazz combo, and, if you actually learn how to scat, you can sing with us. Poor Tina, can't sing and play flute at the same time. Our first rehearsal is tomorrow." He took out the old duffel bag.

"When do you think we'll be ready to perform?" I said.

This time, Marsha answered my email immediately. I thought she'd be her frenzy-eyed self the night before their spring show. I should have known she was a professional. I imagined her phone buzzing and flashing as she corrected each singer's sway, urging more spontaneity.

"I may have graduated, but I will always be here for Voices of Reason," Marsha said. She touched up her stage makeup without a mirror, sliding wax on her eyebrows. "You did practice, right?"

I know nobody goes to shows for the opening act. Victor, Tina, a bass, and I hadn't practiced as much as I told Marsha. The singer stands in front. I blinked away sun while the instruments tuned up. I didn't have to come into the music. No cue to tip me or anyone else. Every person I saw sitting. Dorm, fellows, class, teacher, others. Who are all these people? The circles diffused out without end. I blinked them away, too.

## Chapter 24

I guess it's the kind of feeling people get at weddings or would have gotten at their funerals. It was a small ceremony. I hadn't told any of them, didn't think we were really friends. But they pumped their arms and whooped, cheering and laughing when they saw me seeing. It doesn't take much to show up. One evening for an acquaintance becomes somebody else's kindling, many dry years later. I still don't know who they are. I keep doing this to myself, sorting people by shape and classifying them, each into their own stratum with its own suffocating circle. I don't know how to stop. I thought if I primped the past I'll have more to keep, but maybe in the telling of things I've lost corners like my mother does. Symbolism and endings weren't my life that year. People don't have good-byes in real life. They have partings that they pretend. But it's all so pretty now; I can't throw them away.

Sometimes I think these friends are facts of a moment I could only touch when I was freshly broken. I guess healing is a kind of closing off, or it has been for me. The cracks already sealed over, and I have less room inside. That year and those people still come to me with the radiance of disbelief, the exhilaration that I was wrong to think myself outside of love. In losing desperation, maybe I lost the openness that comes with emptiness, the hungering to be filled. Or maybe I haven't been in the right places or met the right people.

For years, I never had a picture, because I hated to take away any of his texture. Who needs a photo when you have one good look smashed in lights? And now he's finally paper. I'll read if I forgot.

I used to think I couldn't improvise, because I wouldn't be able to forget the old tunes. I'd get trapped into singing along. I clear my throat and make the clearing into a kind of song, fight to keep its melody from turning into another. The spotlights kick, the horn blares, and Arthur's dancing, from the front row. On the other side, sun meets land. I follow as long as I see. I think he thought I found him the whole time. I don't know how long he danced like that. My laugh was running into the scat, looping until I felt an end. Seeing him again, I learn that all old music comes back a million times. The remembering and mingling multiply each word into orchestra, every clatter, until voices inside and outside build one original minute.

He died early, later that year. Three years alone until graduation, seven alone years after. Another long walk, across another frozen stage, for a paper he'll never read. He won't be on the other side this time. I never stop missing him, the years on my own. It's not enough. We ran out. I was late again. I tried to follow you, like I promised. I did write it all down, what I could remember. I guess it wasn't much, our year. It will be less when I wake up.

I try to remember our last talk, and I'm relieved it has slipped away. I forget most of our conversations, but I don't make up the feeling. Our friendship was a light thing. To weigh down the moments takes away the gold. It never has to fade if I forgot. It will be enough, when I wake up, to remember you.

I'll hurry up, write faster, find you again and again. And if I can't read, I'll tell them to read to me faster. Who cares about the beginnings of things? I went the wrong way anyway. I wouldn't trade you for anybody else. I was wrong to want a different end.

When I wake up, I'll tell them, skip to our chapter, our story. I know you'll wait. I don't need to know where it went, our tree, your house, our memories, my mind. Your face has gotten wiser over the years, less ordinary than it was to start and always. I'll read our book, I promised. It will be my first

## Chapter 24

and last thought. I'll read it again and again. I'll meet you again and again. I'll remember our eyes meeting many times: they are the same color and quality. You weren't my first love, but you are the one who sticks.

# SUMMER: SOMETHING WHOLE

# Chapter 25

When we got to her graduation, everybody was talking about Heidi. Her friends wrapped her in a queen's robe, with fake fur spiky as a tortoise. Tita May gave her a crown of starred tinsel. She went to a huge high school, so it felt like she was at the other end of a telescope. From a far distance, she could have been a real royal or prime minister at least. I know valedictorian speeches are mostly terrible; I know mine was. I remember Heidi's being original. She talked about originality, upcoming scientific discoveries, a lot about the irreversibility of choices. I'm not sure if I totally agree, but it was true in a literal sense and in an endings sense.

I sat with my mother and Scott. Tita May bought a new camera for the occasion and was crawling, pivoting at the base of the stage with other overly emotional parents. I thought she'd lie down on the grass in a minute, take an angle of Heidi as a looming titan, and I was relieved that she was just crouching. Heidi saw her and laughed in the middle of her speech. Tita May got the shot.

My mother found a loose spot, pinched my arm, and settled her head on my shoulder.

"You did it, *anak*," my mother said. "Next will be your own graduation." She was right, and I knew it then.

We waited for Heidi at the end of the line of graduates, trying to keep modest expressions since everybody knew who we were. Or if they didn't, they soon found out from everyone's congratulations. It was fun trying to keep straight faces. I thought I was good at it. Heidi finally arrived in a canopy of glory that her friends carried with equal humility. Tita May encouraged Heidi to turn to her friends and talk gibberish for a candid photo. Scott asked an admirer to take photos of the family, and Heidi reached into the pocket of her black robe. She showed us the unmistakable ticket.

"Thank you for everything, Ma. Today is your day, too," Heidi said. She hugged her mother. "I love you. Look, we got you a graduation present. Plane tickets. You can go to the Marcelo reunion now."

Tita May held the ticket down and away, like it was a glassed insect. "We didn't tell you girls enough," she said. She didn't look at my mother, only at the words, which she read again and again.

"You're coming with me," she said to Heidi.

"We only bought one ticket," I said.

"Martha, don't be crazy. Listen to me. Science can wait. It's not going anywhere, is it?" Tita May said. "You'll come with me, Erning, and I'll show you. Before you leave me, we need to go home."

Her bracelets wink when she waves away Heidi's plans, shooing a contingent future for a known love. She knows what they need. But she leaves a hand open for her to choose.

Heidi's mouth lifts, begins, closes. She slams her eyes for a minute. Underneath, her eyes scan her mother and her future, round and tough as seeds. I can't help her because time travel shows what you did, not what you lost. Her mother keeps looking, and Heidi's losing two joys at once, the joining and the beginnings of things.

## Chapter 25

Tita May will take it back if Heidi keeps on, and I can already see Heidi's doubt budding in the other. Her eyes are retaking their old opacity. They will be too far to spark. Heidi swallows, breathes, hard and sharp. I watch her choose her life.

You have to do something. A shadow comes over Heidi's face. For this is the comet's tail, the end of holidays, the last summer. In the air, I see rocks the size and brilliance of planets, aflame even as they curve, reversing gravity from the sun to the earth. How do you stop a comet from crashing? It's been a rough go, this season of showers, meteors smoking to ashes by the time they hit me.

But they could still bounce, more plastic than they looked. If I find a pocket deep enough, the dead rocks will erupt again on their own. Before their gases cool, settle, explode. Or after. They'll find the flashpoint they had that year. It wouldn't be the first time.

The electricity might ignite or burn. I could have stars or cinders. Nobody knows.

And even if she goes, won't she wonder what she missed? Or is waiting the worse wonderment? I have to do something.

Even if she goes, she'll still need to pack, drive, and stand. She'll still need to wait. It'll be crowded, with too many people she can't refuse. I'll have to smile through the nerves, the voltage. And that moment, when the chair kicks back and my eyes close, I don't know if I can last. How do you prepare the thoughts you want?

I wrote my way back into my life, like I wanted. It's paper now. And if I can't read, people will read to me. I kept some. And if I never wrote, I kept some. Some of myself stuck and woke up with me. I'll find it again, I'll have a reunion again, for all the days I need, even if I don't know. I'll take a walk with my story, follow the faces I've seen before, until we sail against the bats all the way home. I will be a navigator before maps. I can't get lost because the people will lead me where I need to go.

The chair kicks up again. She sits up, looks around. At the end, her trip contracts. She could wake up to a new order of things, whether worse or better, and she won't remember all of what came before. I know all that already. She can't lose what she forgot. I had so many plans. She'll lose them, too, no matter what she decides, because she planted the seed in her pocket, and it could grow into anything, like anything else.

I hope she goes. I hope I do something. We can only ready so much, pack what we can carry, take as much of ourselves as we can hold. Our friends take the rest. Don't forget, they live at both ends. And she has to wake up either way. And she has to wait either way. I can't have another day with the same sun. I'll wait for her, between the slamming and re-opening. And if I'm here when she wakes up, I'll tell her that the first and last thoughts don't count. Turn your eyes away from the electric lights, back into the body where you have always been home.

# Acknowledgments

In writing this book, I enjoyed going back to my college times, especially my own third freshman year. I have too many acknowledgments, but I'm going to embrace the beauty of self-publishing and not hold back. Thank you to the characters who helped me graduate and tell this story.

*Cosmin*: My husband, for all of our days, especially for your time creating our book

*Claire*: My friend and editor, for honoring our book

*Tim, Amanda, and Tita Nannette*: For your excitement before you met the book, for your help after you read

*Mom, Dad, Nanay, Lolo Che, Mommy Laly, and Daddy Nap*: For giving me life, for the stories and all the books, for the revolution

*NJ, Mabel Ann, Karen, Jenny, and John*: When you were born, I got one more best friend

*Krystle, Maggie, and Jackie*: My kindred spirits, who loved and understood me first

*Grady*: Friend of my life, you teach me about love

*Terry McGinn and Betty Jo Azpell*: For believing in all of your students, for giving me enough happy experiences that made my later recovery possible

*Ninang Agnes and Ninong Arnel*: For loving me, especially for hosting me in Los Angeles

*Tito Gani, Tita Judy, and Kovu*: My family at Stanford, for welcoming me into your home again and again

*Sara*: For our tower room, our fun, our summer, staying my friend, and making me hang out with Cosmin

*Danny and Steven*: My summer crew, for helping me when I almost failed school, got evicted, and got married

*Brittany*: Half of the best roommate pair, for helping me finally finish freshman year, for showing me that writers are real people

*Jonathan*: My day one buddy

*Mindy*: My partner in fun and joyful discovery, for making me believe again in the possibility of dreams

*Chuck*: For inspiring me to advocate and live well for others, for all the laughs

*Pastor Greg*: My role model for wholly participating in the life of a community, for our teamwork in two most memorable adventures

*Madiha*: My first friend of adulthood, for teaching me about friendship throughout life

*Dr. Leahy*: For your kindness and healing

*Bill*: The one who sticks

Marie Deaconu-Baylon was born in Manila, Philippines and grew up in Wisconsin. Marie studied Philosophy as an undergraduate at Stanford University. She earned a master's degree from University of Chicago School of Social Service Administration. Marie lives in Chicago with her Romanian-American husband and manic depression.

Made in the USA
San Bernardino, CA
29 May 2017